POISONED POLITICS

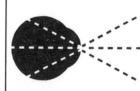

This Large Print Book carries the
Seal of Approval of N.A.V.H.

POISONED POLITICS

MAGGIE SEFTON

THORNDIKE PRESS
A part of Gale, Cengage Learning

GALE
CENGAGE Learning®

Detroit • New York • San Francisco • New Haven, Conn • Waterville, Maine • London

GALE
CENGAGE Learning·

LIBRARY OF CONGRESS CATALOGING-IN-PUBLICATION DATA

Sefton, Maggie.
    Poisoned politics / by Maggie Sefton. — Large print edition.
        pages ; cm. — (Thorndike Press large print mystery) (A Molly Malone
    mystery)
    ISBN-13: 978-1-4104-6391-3 (hardcover)
    ISBN-10: 1-4104-6391-5 (hardcover)
    1. Murder—Investigation—Fiction. 2. Political fiction. 3. Large type books.
    I. Title.
    PS3619.E37P65 2013b
    813'.6—dc23   2013033753

Published in 2014 by arrangement with Midnight Ink, an imprint of
Llewellyn Publications, Woodbury, MN 55125-2989 USA

Printed in the United States of America
1 2 3 4 5 6 7 18 17 16 15 14

To my four daughters —
Christine, Melissa, Serena, and Maria —
who have always believed in me and
supported my work.

Thank you, girls.

ONE

Summer heat in Washington, D.C., is unlike any other. It brushes against the skin velvet-soft, seductive. When first stepping out into a midsummer morning, that velvet caress sidles up beside you, tempting you to linger outside.

"Walk with me," it whispers. "Stay awhile. See how nice it is, here in the shade."

Beguiled, you stay, and before you know it, you've walked blocks along shady avenues. The brief warning bursts of heat at intersections, ignored. Shade beckons across the street again. Not noticing the sheen on your skin or the dampness of fabric, you linger. "A little longer," it whispers. Seduced yet again, you stay.

Not unlike the city of Washington itself. Its seductive whisper can enthrall for a lifetime. Before you know, twenty years have passed in summer's languorous heartbeats.

Politicians and the press are especially vulnerable, as is anyone who works within sight of Capitol Hill and Congress. For them, the enchantment is particularly strong. The whiff of power is an intoxicating perfume. Some can break free. Others cannot. They die here, even if the burial is delayed for years.

Some of us are lucky. We suddenly find ourselves out of that seductive summer shade and standing in the brutal noontime sun — sunburned and sweating and wondering how we got there. Walk outside in the dog days of summer? *Are you crazy?*

That was precisely what I was thinking as I stood at the corner of Wisconsin Avenue and M Street, waiting to join the throngs of tourists to cross the main intersection of Georgetown. Most of them were prepared for their summer visit to Washington, with sun hats, fanny packs, and water bottles. What I wouldn't give for one of those water bottles, but I was too rushed to stop for one now.

Why I'd chosen to walk down to the Georgetown Mall on my lunch hour, I didn't know. It had been one of those partly cloudy, sultry mid-July mornings when I left my office at Senator John Russell's home. The shady Georgetown streets beckoned, and I decided to squeeze in a lunchtime visit to the high-rise Georgetown shopping mall.

Unfortunately, when I'd emerged from the mall's air-conditioned cocoon, the sun glare was brutal. My new royal blue silk blouse was drenched, and I'd only been walking five minutes. I'd look like a dishrag by the time I returned to the Russell mansion. *What was I thinking?* I should have saved the shopping until later in the evening.

However, this evening I was already meeting my old friend Samantha Calhoun at her McLean, Virginia, home. Picturing an icy martini waiting for me, I joined the tourist throng and traipsed across the street when the light changed. My cell phone's music barely penetrated the street noise surrounding me, but my ears had grown even sharper these last four months of working for the Independent junior senator from Colorado. I retrieved the phone from my purse once I reached the curb.

"Molly, where are you?" Peter Brewster's voice even cut through Wisconsin Avenue traffic. "We need you here now."

"I'm on my way, Peter," I said to Russell's chief of staff as I picked up my pace along the avenue, the package banging into my hip as I walked. "I ran down to the shops on lunch. I figured you and the senator would be on your way to the airport like usual on a Friday. What's up?"

"No trip to Colorado this weekend. Russell just got a call from the Majority Leader. Stanley appointed him to Karpinsky's vacancy on the Senate Banking, Housing, and Urban Affairs Committee."

That caught me up short. I stopped so abruptly on the sidewalk that a guy nearly ran into me from behind. "*What!* I can't believe that!"

"Neither did I at first, but I'll fill you in when you get here. Hop in a cab and hurry back. I need to go over some things before the senator and I head back to the Hill."

"Okay, flagging down one now," I said, ending the call as I stepped off the sidewalk to wave at a passing taxi. He ignored me. *Damn.* I guess I'd have to do the Death Wish hail as I stepped farther into traffic and prayed a delivery truck wouldn't run me over.

"That is one plum assignment. The Majority Leader is obviously trying to woo Senator Russell into the Democratic fold permanently," I said, following Peter from my office into the mansion hallway. Polished walnut floors stretched to the front entry doors.

"That's what the Senator and I figured," Peter said, as he texted a message while striding down the hallway. Me, I had to slow down and text, otherwise the message would be gibberish.

Tall, silver-haired, and distinguished, Senator Russell appeared at the end of the hallway. I zipped around still-texting Peter to catch the senator before he answered the ringing Blackberry in his hand.

"Congratulations, Senator. That's fantastic news!" I said as I strode up, hand outstretched.

Russell grabbed my hand in his huge paw and shook it vigorously. "Thank you, Molly. We'll have more time to talk tomorrow night. I'm inviting the entire staff from the Hill here to celebrate, and I have forbidden Luisa to lift a finger," he said, smiling at his housekeeper of nearly forty years. "The caterers will handle it all."

"Sounds great, Senator, but right now you'd better lift a finger and answer that phone. Could be Majority Leader Stanley," I teased, pointing at the still-buzzing phone in his hand.

Russell flashed his huge grin. "Just finished talking with him, Molly." He clicked a button on the phone. "This is Senator Russell," he said into the phone as he headed through the open door Luisa held for him.

Peter followed behind. "Text me when you've sent those e-mails we talked about. And check with Annie at the Hill office on tomorrow night's dinner. She's handling arrangements." Peter looked over his phone at me, brow furrowed. "There was something else."

"Don't worry about it. Text me when you remember it later." I pushed him toward the still-open door. "Albert's revving up the engine. Get out of here."

Peter scurried out the front door and down the steps to the sidewalk leading to the driveway.

"Is there anything I can get you, Molly?" Luisa said as she closed the door.

"Just keep that coffee coming, Luisa. Peter left me a list as long as my arm." I headed to my walnut-paneled office at the end of the hallway.

I slipped off my heels and stretched my legs on the floral-print-covered hassock, then took a deep drink of my martini. *Ohhhh, yes.* Samantha did know how to mix a drink, no matter what the poison.

"Oh, my, that's exactly what I needed," I said, sinking back into one of the cushioned chairs on Samantha Calhoun's screened porch. Another icy sip, and I felt the day's scorching heat fade into memory. "You're still the best bartender this side of the Potomac, Samantha."

"Thank you, sugar," Samantha's lilting Mississippi accent floated through the humid early evening languor. She lifted the cut crystal glass to her red lips and took a deep drink of her favorite bourbon. "You do look a little frazzled. Usually it's quiet over at the Russell Ranch by Friday evening. Didn't the senator head for Colorado this weekend?"

I tasted the delicious flavors of my Cosmo and listened to the cicadas buzzing in the tall oak trees bordering Samantha's backyard. The droning sound rose and fell as other cicadas picked up the refrain and started their own chorus, some higher pitched than the others, some lower. Cicada harmony. I'd missed that distinctively summer sound. Sea level sound, that is. We didn't have cicadas in Colorado. Like a lot of insects, cicadas couldn't live at those higher, drier altitudes. Colorado had less-pleasant pine bark beetles that munched away on our pine trees — and didn't make a sound.

"No, he didn't go to Colorado this week-end, as a matter of fact."

"Well, that's a first. Russell's been a poster boy for tending to his constituents ever since he came here last January. What happened to make him change his plans?"

Samantha had the best instincts of anyone in this city. Sometimes I was convinced she could read my mind, which was seriously scary. "Right as usual, Miss Thing. Russell's got much more important meetings here in town this weekend." I deliberately didn't elaborate, savoring the one time I knew something that Washington-seer Samantha didn't.

"Come on, Molly. You haven't given me any really good intel since you came back to town last March. You owe me, girl." Samantha gave one of her trademark smiles and brushed her auburn hair back from her face.

The vodka tempted me to tease. "Whenever there was something that wasn't privileged, I let you know."

"Tiny morsels. My mice find more than that on their coffee breaks. Now, what's Russell up to? Who's he meeting with?"

I took another sip just to make her wait, picturing Samantha's network of Congressional staffers, assistants, higher-ups, and spouses — her mice, as she called them. They were the reason she managed to stay on top of all political news despite her powerful elderly senator husband's death several years ago.

"Come on, Molly. You know I'll get it out of you."

"Russell got a call from Majority Leader Stanley today. He's been offered Karpinsky's spot on the Senate Banking, Housing, and Urban Affairs Committee."

Her big blue eyes popped wide, clearly surprised. That didn't happen often with Samantha. I exulted inwardly that I'd been able to surprise her. She set her crystal glass down on the end table. "Well, now . . . that *is* a juicy morsel, indeed. In fact, it's huge. You've redeemed yourself, sugar. Thank you for that." She sent a lazy smile my way.

"I'll wait while you spread the word," I said, then took another sip of vodka and cranberry nectar.

Samantha gave an airy wave of her hand. "This will only take a second." She reached for her phone on the coffee table.

"Who's the lucky mouse who'll get the news first?"

Samantha's manicured fingertips sped across the miniature keyboard. "Oh, I have my lieutenants, who've been helping me longer than anyone else." She tossed the little phone aside and reached for her drink.

"Lieutenants, huh? I didn't know your mice could rise in the ranks."

"Battlefield promotions," she said with a grin.

I threw back my head and laughed, feeling the vodka rush through my veins as I remembered a similar conversation. "Danny once told me the same thing when we were at Dumbarton Oaks listening to Ambassador Holmberg talk about international finance. I'd spotted Jed Molinoff in the crowd and started tracking him. Danny was a big help with logistical support." I snickered over my glass. "He promoted me to corporal after that mission."

Samantha stared off into her backyard. Twilight was creeping around the edges of the bushes and trees. In between the Summer Solstice and the Fall Equinox, darkness inched closer each night. Since summer was my favorite season, I chose to ignore the creeping changes. Fall could wait.

"I was surprised that Jed's suicide and affair with Karen didn't stay front-page news for long. After his funeral, it was like the press forgot about him."

"His family was luckier than most," I said,

the memory of my niece Karen dying at Jed's hands diluted the vodka in my veins and brought back my own ugly memories of my husband's death. "When Dave killed himself, it was red meat for the press for a long time."

Samantha glanced over at me. "It's best to let those tortured souls rest in peace. Don't stir up old ghosts. You've finally started a new life here in your old hometown. You should be looking forward, not back into the past. That's how I handle the losses."

I swirled the remaining Cosmo in my glass. Samantha was right. She knew as much about losing loved ones as I did. Her young Navy pilot husband was shot down in Vietnam. Mine shot himself in the head a few years later. Hounded by the jackals that lurked at the edges of Congress. Not every enemy was found in foreign jungles. I took another deep drink and sent those old memories slithering back into the bushes where they belonged.

"You're right. Thanks to this job with Senator Russell, I really feel like I've made a fresh start here. Even though there are ghosts and memories around every corner." I drained my glass and set it on the coffee table.

"I'd say retired colonel DiMateo has helped you concentrate on the future. Is he still away on one of those assignments of his?"

"He said he might be back this weekend," I said as Samantha scooped up my glass and walked to the small bar she kept on the patio porch. God forbid we have to go far for the liquor.

I settled into the cushions, preparing for Samantha's customary grilling on the status of my relationship with my old high school friend. Danny had found me right after I returned to Washington, thanks to my photo that appeared in a sleazy local rag, the *D.C. Dirt*. So much for flying beneath Washington's radar.

Samantha handed me a re-filled glass. "Well, whenever that former Marine returns, you two need to get down to business." She sank back into the cushioned loveseat. "You've been seeing each other for over three months now."

I took a sip and decided to tease. "Off and on. Whenever he's in town. He travels a lot."

"Well, all the more reason for you two to get it on when he's here. Give him some incentive to stay home." She winked before returning to her favorite bourbon.

I laughed out loud. The truth was that

Danny's frequent absences were the only way I'd been able to keep from taking that next step. Why I was hesitating, I wasn't entirely sure.

"I cannot believe he hasn't made a move on you yet."

I grinned at my old friend. Samantha and I had met as teenagers years ago. We'd both been senator's daughters, thus our behavior was always under scrutiny. Both of us were rebels at heart who couldn't afford to be openly rebellious. Our fathers were two of the most powerful men in the U.S. Senate. Consequently, we were watched, despite our best efforts to escape the scrutiny.

"I credit it to Marine Corps discipline."

"Discipline, my ass. He's waiting for a signal. Good God, girl! What're you saving it for?"

I laughed and laughed until tears came to my eyes. "God, Samantha . . . I don't know," I said when I caught my breath. "I don't know why I haven't."

"I know why. You're scared. Scared of jumping into the deep end of the pool again."

I pondered her astute assessment. Trust Samantha to be able to zero in and hit the target. That girl's aim was unerring.

"Yeah . . . maybe you're right. I don't

know if I want to get into the water again."

"Bull," Samantha pronounced in her magnolia-dipped voice. Somehow the word sounded almost proper when she said it. "You're just afraid of getting involved with Danny, that's all. I can tell you care about him. A lot. And I've seen the way he looks at you. That night he picked you up here, I watched the two of you together. You two give off sparks." She tossed down the last of her bourbon and headed for the patio bar again.

"You're right as usual, Miss Thing. I'm afraid if I jumped into the pool with Danny, I might drown in that deep water. He stirs up things inside I haven't felt in years. And yes, that does scare me."

She gave me a sympathetic smile. "Don't worry, sugar. You know how to swim. Go ahead, jump in. The water's fine. I'll be standing by to throw you a life preserver if you need it." She laughed that low sultry laugh of hers as she settled into her chair.

I joined in her laughter. "I'll remember that. We've both survived a lot over the years, Samantha. We're battle scarred, but still standing. To us." I held up my glass, then drained it. "By the way, how's your scintillating liaison going with that Ohio congressman you've taken under your wing.

Quentin Wilson, right?"

"Swimmingly," she teased with a wicked grin. "We've spent some glorious weekends at my Winchester retreat."

I remembered Samantha's country house nestled in the rolling Virginia hills west of the Washington Metro area. Horse country. Dave and I had enjoyed many wonderful parties there years ago. That was when Samantha and her elderly husband, the Senior Senator from Alabama, Beauregard Calhoun, dominated Washington's party scene. Their close-in McLean, Virginia, home was large but not enough to entertain on Beauregard Calhoun's grand scale.

"Boy, you two must rattle around that estate mansion all by yourselves, except for the help."

"I let the staff have the weekends off whenever Quent and I are there. I want to show him what our hot, humid Washington summers are good for. And we need privacy." She winked at me over her glass.

I matched Samantha's low laughter. "You are truly heartless. Torturing that unsuspecting Ohio innocent like that. You know no shame."

"Actually, he's not so innocent. He's been indulging in discreet affairs ever since he first came to Washington four years ago. Apparently he and his wife have an arrangement. She doesn't mind as long as he stays out of the papers. She comes from old Ohio money and cuts a swath on the Cleveland social scene. She comes to Washington once a month."

I'd heard stranger arrangements than that over the years. "That's convenient, I guess," I said with a little shrug. "Well, when he starts 'making his mark,' I imagine his wife will want to jump into the scene here. But I'm sure you would have cut him loose by then, right?"

Samantha swirled the bourbon in her glass. "Probably."

That answer got my attention even through the vodka. "Probably? That doesn't sound like your usual operating procedure. What's up with this guy, Miss Thing? Does he need more coaching than normal?"

She looked out into the backyard, her teasing smile missing. "In a manner of speaking. Quent's smart as a whip, smarter than a lot of his House colleagues. But he can also be a little obsessive sometimes. I mean, when he delves into some subcommittee topic, he keeps on digging. Keeps his office staffers overtime. He's like a dog with a bone and doesn't know how to pace himself yet. He's going to wear himself out or cut his own throat by annoying senior congressmen."

"Hmmmmm. That's a fine line. He'll either learn to walk it, or he'll find no allies when he needs them." I recognized some of that behavior from my young husband's passion for pursuing a subject dear to his heart years ago. A worthy trait until you stepped on powerful toes. The U.S. House of Representatives was filled with senior congressmen who held the most powerful positions on certain committees.

"I know. That's why he worries me, Molly. I confess Quentin has gotten to me more than any other of my . . . uh, pupils."

I stared at Samantha. I had never heard her say that about any of the casual liaisons she'd had since her husband died. Old recently departed friends like Senator Sol Karpinsky were in a different category.

"Well, I can't think of anyone better to coach Congressman Wilson the art of moderation than you." I sent my old friend a warm smile. I sensed Quentin Wilson had gotten to Samantha despite her vow to not become personally involved. We were all human, therefore, susceptible. The heart knew no rhyme or reason.

Samantha met my gaze. "Thanks, Molly. I appreciate that."

"And if necessary, I'll stand beside the deep end of the pool and throw you a life preserver if you need it," I repeated her promise to me.

"I assume all systems are good to go?" Raymond's scratchy voice came over the cell phone.

"Of course," the sandy-haired man replied, breaking his long stride as he ran along the trail beside the Potomac River. Friday night, and less runners were out. The late-day July heat kept the weak-willed away.

"I know I don't need to ask, but the higher-ups need reassurance."

"Understandable, at these rates." The man chuckled as he settled on a cement bench set back from the water. Directly across the river, East Potomac Park stretched out. Rugby and soccer teams were scrimmaging in the early evening twilight.

"Any security at her place?"

"Just run-of-the-mill, several years old. I checked it out the other day when she and her housekeeper were gone. No problem getting the codes."

"Excellent. We don't want any unexpected problems. I promised Spencer this would all go like clockwork. Are the packages ready for tomorrow?"

"Yes. Both local and Ohio special delivery."

Raymond chuckled. "By the way, those were some great photos. They'll definitely get his attention."

"You can't beat digital," the man joked.

Raymond's loud laughter came over the phone, followed by a wheezing cough.

TWO

Saturday

I sipped the last of my morning coffee as I stood by my kitchen window. I'd grown familiar with the regular morning flow of people passing my Georgetown townhouse on P Street, hurrying to work on weekdays or hurrying somewhere else on weekends. Even mothers pushing baby strollers seemed in a hurry. Nobody strolled anymore. Of course, I seldom strolled either. So I couldn't fault everyone else for rushing about when I succumbed to the same behavior.

Even though it was Saturday, I'd be rushing to the Russell mansion as soon as I finished my coffee. Tonight was Senator Russell's celebration dinner, and the house would be packed. But that was nothing compared to the congratulatory messages that would be waiting via e-mail, texts, and phone once I got to my office. I'd be working all day.

I rinsed my empty coffee cup, grabbed my briefcase, and headed out the front door. The large, striped tabby cat that camped out every day beside my terraced brick flower beds glanced lazily over his shoulder and meowed.

"Hey, Bruce. Watch over everything while I'm gone," I said racing down the brick steps leading to the sidewalk below. "And leave those birds alone."

Bruce gave me one of those inscrutable kitty smiles in reply. Where Bruce lived, I hadn't a clue, but he appeared in my front yard daily. He was a big tomcat. Not fat, but muscular, which made his owner's choice of a name even more incongruous. A couple of months ago, I'd checked his license and ID tags and was surprised to see only his name engraved. No owner's name nor address, not even a phone number. Apparently Bruce's owner didn't care if he returned or not.

I headed down P Street, careful to avoid the broken sections of brick pavement that jutted upward, waiting to send someone sprawling. I'd been living in this lovely and exclusive neighborhood ever since I began working for Senator Russell in March. The townhouse Peter Brewster let me use rent-free was only three blocks from Senator Russell's mansion, so I'd been walking to and from work every day.

I thoroughly enjoyed the morning walk through Georgetown's historic shady streets, lined on both sides with beautiful examples of Federal and Georgian architecture. Later designs were also present, but my tastes ran to the earlier periods. That bias came from being a Virginian and living in a state filled with former Presidents' mansions. A great many of Georgetown's period homes bore the metal plaques identifying them as belonging to the National Historic Register. History was all around on these streets. Inescapable.

My cell phone's distinctive music sounded. Rolling Stones, "Brown Sugar." Since this was my personal line, I figured I could indulge my rock 'n' roll addiction. Plus, it was fun watching people's reactions if they heard it. I dug the phone out of my purse and let a few seconds of guitar riffs disturb the Georgetown quiet as I walked along. Danny's name appeared on the cell phone screen, and my pulse sped up.

"Hey, you're back early," I said, unable to disguise the pleasure in my voice. *Why would I want to?*

"I'm not back yet, but it's getting closer. I

thought I'd give you a call and see what you're up to. You going over to visit your cousins this weekend?"

"I haven't decided yet. This whole weekend is turned around. Russell's staying in town and we're hosting a dinner tonight for his entire staff, here and on the Hill. Everyone. It's going to cost a fortune."

Danny chuckled. "Ever the accountant, right? Relax and enjoy it, Molly. What's up? Russell usually heads to Colorado each weekend."

"We're celebrating tonight. Yesterday Senate Majority Leader Stanley offered Russell the vacant seat on the Senate Banking, Housing, and Urban Affairs Committee. Sol Karpinsky's old seat."

Danny whistled. "Sweet. That's quite a coup for Russell."

"My words exactly. I'm sure the Democrats are gambling this plum assignment will guarantee Russell voting with them. But that gamble probably won't pay off. Russell's his own man and determined to stay Independent. He'll vote with them sometimes and other times, not."

"That's my kind of senator. Hat's off to Russell. I'll bet Brewster is running in six directions at once."

"Ohhhh, yeah." I laughed as I turned onto

30th Street, angling toward Q Street. "And I'll be buried on the computer answering all those e-mails."

"Listen, where do you want to go to dinner when I return?" Danny's voice had dropped into that low tone that always made my heart skip.

Your place, Crazy Ass tempted.

McDonald's, Sober-and-Righteous countered. *Bright lights. Lots of people. Safer.*

I ignored the two competing voices inside my head. Crazy Ass, the wild, go-for-it voice, was getting stronger lately, I'd noticed. But good old watchdog Sober-and-Righteous could usually be counted on to throw cold water on any untoward suggestion. Boring as hell, but dependable, was Sober.

"Ahhhhh, I don't know," I demurred. "You pick."

"Okay, I have a new place in mind over on Connecticut. I think you'll like it. Great Indian food and excellent wines."

"Plus several of those yummy desserts I can't resist like Gulab Jamun." I pictured the delicious and deadly golden confection saturated in sugar syrup and rose water. For someone like me with a sweet tooth, it was heavenly.

"I'll take that as a yes."

"Absolutely, Squad Leader," I said as I pushed open the Russell mansion's wrought iron front gate. "Hey, I've arrived at Russell's. I'll text you after that huge dinner is over. Let you know how it went."

"Roger that."

"Try not to do anything really scary dangerous," I joked.

"I'll take it under advisement." He paused, then added in that low voice. "By the way, I miss you."

I stopped in the middle of the mansion's front steps, pulse racing, and not from the steps. I pondered what to reply, when Crazy Ass spoke up for me.

"Roger that." I clicked off before he could say more.

Leaning on the doorway to the Russell kitchen, I watched the catering staff stream in and out of the kitchen from their truck in the back driveway. Pushing metal carts loaded with rectangular metal serving pans, carrying empty coffee urns and cartons of fresh berries and vegetables, everyone on the caterer's staff was busy.

Senator Russell's housekeeper Luisa ruled the Russell kitchen and stood in the corner overseeing the proceedings and preparations. Her husband, Albert, was Russell's

31

longtime chauffeur and had been running errands non-stop all morning. The Senator and Peter would return about an hour before everyone was due to arrive.

Sunlight poured through the wide upper windows, bathing the kitchen in bright light. I took a sip of Luisa's strong dark coffee and watched the catering staff begin their preparatory routine. I'd seen it so often since late March that I had their routine memorized by now. Part of my duties for Senator Russell was to be the "stand-in" hostess whenever the Senator was delayed. Having grown up in the midst of Capitol Hill politics and Washington parties, it was as natural as breathing for me. My U.S. senator father, Robert Malone from Virginia, entertained often and strategically. Plus, my husband, David Grayson, had served three terms as a rising-star young congressman from Colorado, so the two of us entertained frequently before his future was cut short. Asking me to handle a room full of politicians and political staffers was like telling a duck to leave the pond and go swim in the lake. *Quack, quack.*

Casey Moore, the senator's security guard, joined me in the doorway. The tall, broad-shouldered African-American was a retired career Marine like Danny and had actually served under him in Beirut during those tragic days of 1983. He'd been the one to translate the young lieutenant's nickname, "Double D." Casey said it stood for *Damned Dangerous.* I should have known.

"I can see dollar signs dancing above your head, Molly," Casey teased.

"You bet they are. I shudder to think about the bills." I took another sip of coffee. "At least we finally finished entertaining the Congressional hordes last month. I thought we'd get a breather with only a weekly dinner or two."

Casey chuckled over his coffee mug. "Dream on. You've seen the Senator in action for four months now. You know he thrives on these big events."

"You're right about that," I sighed in resignation as we turned toward the long stretch of walnut hallway.

"Hey, look at it this way," he said as he fell in step beside me. "As long as Russell is entertaining like this, you're guaranteed a job as his accountant." He laughed and saluted me with his mug as he headed toward his post outside in Russell's manicured backyard gardens. His perch on the patio gave him a bird's-eye view of every kitchen worker who scurried from caterer trucks to the kitchen and back.

I continued down the hall, passing the elegant formal living and dining rooms. I noticed that Luisa had placed more fresh flowers in the vases in the living room and the round crystal bowl in the midst of the mahogany dining room table. I turned the corner into my office just in time to hear "Brown Sugar" blasting from my private phone. Samantha's name flashed on the screen as I picked up.

"Hey, how're you doing?" I asked as I sank into the upholstered desk chair. Moving the mouse so I could see how many e-mails had accumulated during my coffee break, I flinched at the number.

"Not good at all, Molly," Samantha said, her voice sounding tight. "I'm mad as hell and getting madder by the minute."

I forgot about the e-mail deluge and swiveled my chair around. "What's the matter? Has something happened?"

"I just got off the phone with Quent Wilson. He called to tell me that he and I had to stop seeing each other. Right now. He had a special delivery this morning. It was a package of 8 × 10 photos. Surveillance photos, if you can believe that. Taken of Quent and me at my Winchester home last month. He could tell from the dates and times on the bottom of the photos."

I set my coffee mug aside as a chill passed over me. *A blackmailer. It had to be.* Everyone in Washington knew that Samantha Calhoun was beyond wealthy. And what had she said last night? Wilson's wife was from "old Ohio money."

Clearly, someone had learned of their affair and was attempting to cash in on that knowledge.

"Oh, my God . . ." I whispered. "What kind of photos? Were they . . ."

"The very worst kind. As I was talking to Quent, a delivery service brought the same package to me. That freak took photos of us in the bedroom!"

"Oh, no . . . Samantha . . . I'm so sorry. That's awful! Was there any note or anything from the person who took the photos? It's got to be a blackmail attempt, don't you think?"

"That's what I thought, but Quent said there wasn't any blackmail note included in his package. And there wasn't one in mine. And neither of us has received any phone calls. Needless to say, Quent is panicking. He's afraid that his wife hired the surveillance."

"Uh oh. I remember you said he and his wife had an arrangement. Do you think she found out about you two and is going to divorce him or something?"

"That's what he's afraid of. And since she's the bankroll behind his campaigns, you can understand his panic. What's worse is he's afraid she'll be vindictive and try to ruin his career by leaking these photos on some sleazy website."

"Oh, no . . ." I breathed, picturing lurid photos showing up online going worldwide in an instant and lasting forever. As long as someone could save them to a file or flash drive, those photos could be used to torment Samantha and Wilson for the rest of their lives.

"Which means I'll be dragged through the mud along with him. *Dammit!*" Samantha said, her voice tight with anger.

"Maybe his wife won't do that. I thought their arrangement was Wilson could see whomever he wanted as long as he didn't get into the papers. The last time I looked, you guys weren't in the *Washington Post* or even the *D.C. Dirt.*"

"Good God, don't even think it."

"You two have been discreet. Neither you nor Wilson has flaunted the affair. So, maybe she just wants to make him squirm. You know . . . show she has power over him."

"Lord, Molly, I hope you're right."

"Has Wilson called his wife? Has he heard anything from her?"

"No. He's afraid to call. He doesn't know what to do, he's so scared. He's gone to the Hill for a scheduled staff meeting. Then he'll come back to my house tonight and retrieve his personal belongings. Damn, this is so . . . so tawdry. How can that woman put herself through a feeding frenzy? The vultures will come after her too."

My first thought returned and pushed itself forward. "Samantha, maybe it isn't Wilson's wife behind this. Maybe it really is a blackmailer."

Samantha's long, tired sigh came over the phone. "I wish to God it was, Molly. A blackmailer is only after money and not out for vindictive pleasure and retribution."

"You need to talk to your lawyer, Samantha."

"That's where I'm heading right after this phone call. I've already called him. We need to have some strategy planned for both scenarios. Vindictive wife or blackmailer. Plus, I don't want to be here when Quent comes. I gave him the house security code and told him I'd be gone all evening. Plenty of time for him to gather any personal belongings."

"Samantha, I don't want you alone tonight. I wish I didn't have this dinner, otherwise you could come over and stay with me."

"Thank you for the offer, but I don't plan to be alone. I'm going to seek additional counsel after I speak with my attorney."

I searched through my memory for the name. "Are you still using Jefferson Carter, Beau's longtime lawyer?"

"Most definitely. Also I've got some old friends in town who've been put through the wringer in the past. I'll need their thoughts on this mess."

"That makes me feel better. You'll need advice from wise and experienced heads to steer your way through this thing. I'll call you when I can steal a moment away from the dinner tonight, okay? And if your old friends aren't available, come on over and stay with me."

"Thank you, sugar, but I'm fairly certain I'll be finishing the evening with one dear gentleman. He and I haven't spent time together in quite awhile. It'll be good to talk with him."

"Okay, but if plans change, don't hesitate to call me. Why don't you call me anyway and let me know how you're doing so I won't worry."

A smile finally appeared in Samantha's

voice. "I'll try. Meanwhile, you take care of Senator Russell's folks tonight, you hear? I'll be okay."

"All right. Take care of yourself, Miss Thing," I said, trying to match her lighter tone.

"Always, sugar." She clicked off.

"Has he received the photos yet?" Spencer's low voice came across the cell phone.

Raymond took a long drag on his cigarette and inhaled deeply. The nicotine cloud both soothed and irritated his ragged throat. "I made sure they were delivered to him before he left for the Hill this morning. Special delivery by a special courier."

"Your man, I assume?

"You assume correctly."

"Good, good. Do you know if he opened the package right away?"

"Yes, he did." Raymond took a sip from his cold coffee and leaned back in his upholstered desk chair. A shaft of late morning sun fell across the worn oriental carpet at his feet. "Wilson inspected the package and went back into his townhouse, then he called Mrs. Calhoun. QuickiExpress delivered her package while they were still on the phone. Let's just say neither of them was very happy." He took a quick drag.

"Your man's been keeping track of Wilson?"

"Absolutely. He bugged the townhouse a month ago when he slipped in to check the computer files. Wilson can't take a leak without us knowing. Don't worry, Spencer. Wilson got your message loud and clear. He called his Hill office and said he'd be a little late." Raymond chuckled low in his throat, risking the start-up of that pesky cough.

"Excellent. I assume everything is ready for tonight. Is your man in position?"

"Affirmative. He just scheduled a courier to hand deliver a note to Wilson at his House office. With all the staffers around, they'll make sure to mention it if any cops question them. A single page of paper and typed message: 'You'll be sorry.' "

An exhale of breath on the other end of the phone. "Good, good. We've put a lot of pieces into motion, Raymond. Everything has to work like clockwork."

"Don't worry, it will. We've already started pushing the dominoes. Everything will fall into place, Spencer. Trust me."

"Oh, we do, Raymond. We do. Call me once it starts."

"Of course."

THREE

Sunday

I grabbed my car keys, purse, and coffee mug, ready to head out my kitchen door to run some errands. Early Sunday morning meant the shopping malls would be relatively calm for a couple of hours. After that, the crowds would arrive in force.

I planned to head right across Key Bridge into Virginia then up the George Washington Memorial Parkway to Chain Bridge Road to the McLean, Virginia, exit. If I was lucky, I'd beat the shopping hordes to Tysons Corner. Since I was joining my cousins Nan and Deb and their husbands in Vienna, Virginia, later that afternoon, I figured Tysons Corner made sense. However, Tysons was one of the busiest shopping centers in Northern Virginia, so you had to be really slippery to not get stuck in traffic jams. Of course, knowing all the surrounding streets and alternate routes helped.

Bruce meowed at me as I walked toward the driveway beside my townhouse. I gave him my regular admonition to leave the birds alone. Bruce simply looked at me, then licked his big paw. As I settled into my car that I'd finally been able to bring from Colorado, I heard the driving beat of "Brown Sugar" coming from my purse. I started the car, ready to begin the tricky process of backing out of the narrow Georgetown rowhouse driveway. By the time I retrieved my phone, Mick Jagger was already in full throat, and Samantha's name flashed on the screen.

"Hey, I'm glad to hear from you," I said when Mick disappeared. "I tried calling last night, but you were obviously still in the midst of counsel. What's the word from the Wise Sage?"

"Molly . . . can you come over to my house right now, please? I need to talk to you," Samantha said in a voice so soft I could barely hear her.

"Samantha, are you all right? What's the matter?" I'd never heard her sound like that before.

"I came home early this morning and . . . and found Quentin dead on my couch. He was just slumped over on the cushions."

An icy chill ran through me and caught in

my throat. "Oh, no . . ." was all I managed to gasp out.

"I thought he was asleep but when I couldn't wake him, I checked his pulse." Samantha's voice caught. "God, Molly, it was awful! There were pills scattered all over the coffee table. The police just left a few minutes ago. The ambulance took him away. *Please,* Molly, can you come over? I need someone I can talk to. Someone I can trust."

"I'm leaving now," I said, backing up quickly. To hell with the grass. "I'll be there in a few minutes. Have you called anyone else?"

"Just my lawyer. Dear God, Molly."

"I'm on my way."

I handed Samantha a ceramic mug of English Breakfast tea then sat on a chair across from hers in her paneled library. The idea of sitting in the living room was out of the question.

"Have you had anything to eat?" I asked before sipping my coffee. "I can make you something."

"I had a croissant and jam before I left Ber . . . my friend's house this morning. I don't think I could eat anything now." She chewed her lip, as she clutched the mug in her lap.

Her nervous behavior was so unlike Samantha that it was striking. I could only remember seeing her this rattled as an adult once before. When I went to see her before she flew off to Mississippi and went into seclusion after her young husband's death. Eddie Tyler had died when his plane was shot down during the Vietnam War. There had never been any indication of remains being found. Samantha was told that the plane wreckage was at the bottom of the Gulf of Tonkin Bay.

"Take a sip of tea. Black, no cream or sugar. It's good for you," I prodded.

"All right." Samantha took a sip then held the mug close to her chest with both hands, as if it were winter instead of mid-July.

"Would you mind my asking some questions?" I ventured. "I want to get this entire scene in my head. I'm still confused about a few things."

She nodded. "Go ahead, Molly. It'll help me remember what I told the police. I need to get it inside my head too."

"When did you come home this morning?"

Samantha took a large sip before answering. "I left D.C. about six a.m. and arrived here around six twenty-five, I think. I turned into my driveway and was surprised to see

44

Quentin's car still there. I'd assumed he'd gathered his things and left by early evening."

"Then, you walked inside?"

She closed her eyes and her voice came out tighter. "Yes. I found him on the sofa. I thought he was asleep and kept calling out his name and telling him to wake up! When he didn't answer, I got this sickening feeling. That's when I checked his pulse and didn't feel it. I even checked his throat. His skin was cold. *He* was cold." She shuddered visibly.

"You said there were pills scattered all over the coffee table. Do you have any idea what kind of pills they were? Had you ever seen him take pills before?"

Eyes wide open now, Samantha nodded and sipped more of the strong tea. "Yes, many times. Quent had trouble sleeping. Some nights he couldn't wind down. Even sex didn't seem to relax him. So he took sleeping pills every night." She stared toward the tall cherry wood bookcases, each shelf filled with books and treasures brought back from her international travels. "Several of the capsules were opened and spilled out beside the bottle of beer. Quentin loved Guinness, so I always kept a few bottles in the fridge for him."

I peered at Samantha. "Why would he open the capsules? If he was intent on killing himself, he'd simply swallow them with the beer, wouldn't he?"

"Lord, Molly, I don't know." She looked away from me. "I cannot imagine why Quent would resort to taking his own life. I mean . . . I told him I'd pay the blackmail money if it came to that. Why would he do it?"

Having walked in after a tragic suicide had taken place years ago, I was still at a loss for an explanation to offer Samantha. "Who knows? I still haven't figured out why Dave killed himself, and it's been over twenty years."

She glanced to me with compassion. "I'm sorry if this brings back ugly memories, Molly."

I shrugged. "That's okay. It was a long time ago, and I've come to the conclusion that none of us can know what's going on inside someone else's head. Sometimes the people we care about the most can deliberately hide their thoughts from us."

"I guess you're right."

An idea came suddenly. "Do you think that blackmailer called Wilson? Maybe he scared him and Quentin panicked."

"I don't know, but I don't like the coincidence of those photos arriving on his doorstep Saturday, and that same night Quentin decides to kill himself."

I didn't like coincidences, either. "I know, it doesn't make sense, considering you'd told him that you would pay any blackmail money. Something else must have scared Wilson. Scared him enough to take his life." Another idea surfaced. "What occurs to me is there was *no* blackmailer. You said Wilson was afraid his wife had ordered the photos. Maybe that's exactly what happened, and she called him to tell him she was dumping him. His worse nightmare. His political career would be over. I mean, if she was that well-connected in Ohio, she could influence the powers-that-be to withdraw their support. Then, she'd withdraw her money. That would finish Wilson politically."

Samantha nodded. "Quentin would be unable to mount a re-election campaign without her money, especially if she was using her influence against him. Quent wouldn't have a prayer. He was a Cleveland D.A. from a modest background. Then he started winning several high-profile cases against some financial con men who'd defrauded scores of Ohioans out of their retirement savings. That's when he got on

47

the Ohio politicos' radar screen. And, caught Sylvia Burnham's eye. She's old Ohio money. After they married, it was an easy climb upward for Quent."

I scrutinized Samantha. "You really did research him, didn't you?"

In a brief return to her old self, Samantha arched a brow at me. "I told you I researched my pupils. I looked for anything that might hold him back or become fodder for the media sleaze."

I leaned back in the chair and sipped my coffee, pondering what she'd said. "You know, I'm thinking more and more that Wilson's wife may have been the one to push him over the edge. I'd be willing to bet she called him while he was still here. And it was a downward spiral for Wilson after that." I took another sip of coffee. "Boy, I wish we knew who called him last night."

Samantha picked at her nails. "Actually I do know who he talked to last night."

"What?" I stared at her.

Samantha stared at her hands. "I . . . I saw his cell phone on the sofa beside him and . . . I went through the phone logs before I called the police."

Whoa. I hadn't expected that. "Wow, that was really clear thinking."

She gave me a worried look. "I know how

that sounds, Molly. But I couldn't help myself. I wanted to know who called Quentin before he did this horrible thing. Someone drove him to suicide, and I want to know who it is."

"Did you recognize any phone numbers?"

"Yes, there was one that matched his home number in Cleveland. I recognized it from my own phone log when he'd call from Ohio." She rose from her chair and went to the small cherry wood desk across the room, then returned with a folded sheet of paper. "I wrote down all the numbers that Quent talked to Saturday afternoon. He said he'd be at the Hill most of the day."

I reached for the paper and scanned the long list of numbers. Since this was Wilson's personal line, the list was shorter than it would have been if constituents were listed. Even so, Samantha had copied an entire column of phone numbers. "These are a lot of calls. Which was his Ohio phone?"

She pointed a fire engine red fingernail at one number. "This one. I checked it with my phone logs, and it's his home. So, that means his wife *did* call him yesterday evening."

I exchanged a glance with Samantha. "The police took his cell phone, right?"

She nodded. "Yes, they did. But I'm not sure they'd bother to check who called Quentin. After all, it's an obvious suicide."

"Maybe, maybe not. Do you recognize any other numbers on this list?"

"Yes, several are from his Capitol Hill office. The rest of them looked like other numbers on the Hill, probably colleagues and staffers. Still, I may give the list to a professional to check to be sure."

"Why?"

Her face darkened. "If it wasn't his wife and he was being blackmailed, one of those numbers could be the blackmailer's. If so, I want to expose the bastard. He was responsible for Quentin killing himself."

"So, you have a private eye on retainer?" I couldn't help smiling.

She sent me one of her looks, which made me feel better. Nervous, hesitant Samantha didn't resemble the woman I'd known for a lifetime. "Molly, there's an awful lot of stuff going on in Washington. Even more than when you lived here. You never know if someone is who he or she says they are. I always have a background check done if I'm going to do business with someone. An expensive suit and a smile aren't enough. Some job histories are suspect. Even personal recommendations can be suspect. I like to know the people I'm dealing with."

"That makes sense. Better safe than sorry."

"Precisely."

I was impressed with Samantha's caution. Sober-and-Righteous prodded that I needed to adopt that attitude myself. I ignored it. Samantha returned to her desk and dropped the folded paper beside a lamp. Then my instinct prodded me. *That,* I listened to.

"You know, you should scan that list into your computer and save it to a file. That way you'll have an electronic copy to send to your investigator guy . . . or girl. Then you could actually destroy that paper list. Better not to have it around."

"Good point." She gave me a smile then reached over and turned on her computer and scanner and settled in her desk chair.

Another concern surfaced and I had to voice it. Samantha needed to prepare herself. "You know the police are going to question you once they find out about your affair with Wilson. You'd better have your story straight."

She glanced over at me with a worried frown. "You're right, and I plan to tell them about the photos and my suspicions about a blackmailer. Besides, they've probably found those photos in Quent's briefcase.

Dear God."

"Are you going to tell them about the arrangement Wilson had with his wife?"

She gave a long sigh. "I will if they ask about his wife. If they don't bring up the subject, I won't go there. What Quentin and his wife, Sylvia, said to each other is their business. It was between husband and wife."

"Okay, but be prepared to tell the truth if they do ask. After all, his wife is probably the one who ordered the photos."

"I know," she said, glancing toward the window.

Another sunny hot summer day lurked outside, waiting for us to step into it. I'd already called my cousins and told them I wouldn't be coming over that afternoon. I didn't want to leave Samantha alone.

"You're staying with me tonight, and I won't take no for an answer. So better pack a bag. Let's get out of here. In fact, it might be better if you didn't stay here until you can have the entire living room area cleaned and redecorated. Change it entirely so it doesn't bring back any memories."

I could see her relax a little. "You're right. I wouldn't be able to sleep anyway. Thank you for asking me over."

"C'mon, let's go pack some bags for you," I said as I rose. Another concern swept forward then, something I had wanted to say earlier but hesitated to do so. "Oh, and you know the police are going to ask you to account for your whereabouts last night, so be prepared to answer. You'll probably have to warn your Wise Sage that he may be questioned too."

She logged out of her computer. "I'm afraid I cannot do that, Molly. Some of my closest gentlemen friends and advisors are rather highly placed in sensitive government positions."

I stared at her, shocked. "Samantha, you have to tell the police where you were! Otherwise they'll suspect you were here with Wilson when he killed himself. And that . . . that could turn ugly. After all, this is your house."

She headed out of her library and down the hall toward the curving staircase leading to the upper floor. "They already asked me where I was last night, and I told them I was with a close personal friend." She started up the stairs and I followed. "Then they asked me the friend's name, and I had to refuse them. I said I promised the gentle-man that I would guard his privacy."

I couldn't believe what I was hearing. "Good Lord, Samantha! You know how that *sounds*? It sounds like you're hiding something. That's bound to make them suspicious."

Samantha was quiet until she reached the top of the stairs. Then she turned and looked at me solemnly. "I cannot help that, Molly. My friend's privacy is very important to me. Besides, it's obvious Quent took his own life. Why would they bother investigating me?"

I followed her down the hallway leading to her bedroom, but a cold feeling started to form in the pit of my stomach.

"Are the police still there?" Spencer asked.

"No, no. They left a couple of hours ago. She must have called it in right after she came home and found him. My man picked up the cop call."

"So far, so good. Now, we have to watch and wait. Make sure this gets handled properly. An accidental overdose. Your man made sure of that, right?"

Raymond sighed. *How many times did he have to go over this?* At these rates, as many times as needed. Billable hours, Washington rates.

"I've told you. He's a pro. He had plenty of time to slip inside and get it done while I distracted Wilson."

"You took a chance, exposing yourself like

that. Besides, it's been years since you've done field work."

Raymond heard the laughter behind the words. "You never lose the knack. You just lose your speed," he joked. "Don't worry. I used an old repairman's uniform in the back of the closet. Big square-brimmed hat. I looked like the Maytag man, I swear to God." Raymond couldn't keep from laughing, despite his cough.

Spencer joined in for a minute. "We may need some media if the investigation drags on. We want this wrapped up and forgotten."

"How about your guy in Congressman Jackson's office? Larry Fillmore. Didn't you say he had contacts with that local rag, *D.C. Dirt*? You might want to start there."

"Yes, he does. Larry's got dirt on everyone." Spencer chuckled. "He's the one who told us about the staffer who delivers. Gary Levitz. In fact, Levitz could turn out to be very useful, indeed. Larry's going to stay in touch with him, just in case we need him later."

Raymond had heard the smug sound to Spencer's voice before. Spencer had found a fall guy.

FOUR

Monday

"Did you read about Congressman Wilson's death in the paper this morning?" Peter Brewster asked as he stepped into my office. "That's tragic. The article didn't say how he died. Of course, that immediately makes a person wonder if he ended his own life."

I took a large drink of coffee before answering. "I read the article, and it does . . . uh, leave some doubts. Did you know him? I confess I don't remember meeting Wilson personally when we entertained the Midwestern congressmen and women a few months ago."

"Yes, I'd met with him a couple of times on the Hill. And his chief-of-staff Natasha Jorgensen. Wilson was one of the sharpest congressmen around." Peter leaned against the doorjamb, his face showing his concern. "He was on the House Energy and Commerce Committee and was working on trade issues. It's a shame to lose him."

"I know. It's tragic to lose talented people in their prime."

"I'm sorry if this dredges up painful memories for you, Molly," he looked at me sympathetically.

"Time has a way of healing over even tragic losses." I said, glancing toward the window, sunshine bathing the Russell garden.

"It's curious, though," he mused. "All the paper said was that he was 'found in a McLean, Virginia, residence.' He must have been visiting a friend, because he has a rowhouse near Capitol Hill."

Peter had just given me the chance to deflect his concentration on Wilson's last hours. "How in the world can you remember where all those congressmen and women live? There're over four hundred of them." I did my best to look amazed.

His familiar grin appeared, changing Peter's boyish face back to the savvy politico look. "I consider that basic intel. Besides, it's really not that hard. So many of them cluster in nearby neighborhoods with their colleagues. If they bring their families with them, then they often move farther out. If they're 'batching' it, they'll get together and share a rowhouse. If they're really scraping by, they'll actually bunk in their offices. The wealthier ones like Wilson can afford classier digs."

I saluted him with my mug. "You're amazing, Peter. Keeping track of the flocks like that. I love your image of shivering congressmen clustering together, like birds in the trees at night trying to stay warm."

He pushed away from my door. "Washington can be a cold place for newcomers. I've learned that. You're established here and have connections, Molly, so you're a lot more comfortable."

"That would be nice if it was true, but this City doesn't care whether you have connections or not. It'll cut you down fast if there's a hint of weakness. There're jackals behind every lamppost, and they can smell even a whiff of blood."

"Cynical already? You've only been back in D.C. a little over four months. Or have you always been that cynical?"

"It's not being cynical. I've simply got my antennae up and my instincts on high alert." I gave him a disarming smile. "Instinct keeps you alive in this town, Peter."

He chuckled. "You scare me sometimes. Listen, there's been a substitution for one of the Senator's dinners in a couple of weeks. Senator Gonzalez and his wife won't be coming. Apparently, there's been a family emergency, and they have to fly back to Arizona. So, I've substituted someone you know quite well. Eleanor MacKenzie."

Eleanor's familiar face came forward in my mind. My elderly advisor and political confidante. Widow of a respected U.S. Senator and Secretary of State, no one was more experienced in the ways of Washington than Eleanor MacKenzie. She had also watched over Samantha and me when we were teenaged Senators' daughters to make sure we stayed out of any semblance of trouble.

"Excellent choice. Eleanor will be a great addition to the group. No one in Washington is more versed in political conversation. No matter what party affiliation, Eleanor is at home."

"I figured you'd approve. After all, you and Eleanor have known each other for ages. If I'm not mistaken, she was something of a mentor."

"Been digging into that notorious file of mine?" I teased. "I should have known."

Peter gave me a wink as he headed into the hallway. "You've got history in this town, Molly. It's inescapable."

Didn't I know it. I sent him a dismissing wave. "Go back to the Hill with the flocks,

Peter, while I bury myself in e-mails."

I settled into my comfy desk chair and returned to my inbox, which bulged once again. *Damn.* I'd just cleared it out. I was only away for a few minutes. Draining my coffee, I debated getting another cup, then decided I had to earn it. *Clear the inbox. Clear the inbox.*

Only five minutes had elapsed — and five e-mails down — when the Stones's driving beat cut through my thoughts. I reached for my personal phone. Samantha's name flashed on the screen.

"Hey, how're you doing?" I asked, anxious to gauge her mood.

"I've been handling phone calls all morning. Once the gossips read that *Washington Post* article saying Wilson was found in a McLean residence, everyone assumed it was my house. I've been fielding inquiries for over two hours." I heard a tired sigh.

"Where are you now?"

"I'm actually still in your kitchen, if you can believe it. But I'm about to shut this phone down, right after I call the interior designer. I've already spoken to my housekeeper. She's arranged for a professional outfit to go through the entire living room. Disinfect it. Then I'm heading over to my lawyer's office again."

60

"Good idea. And you're welcome to stay with me as long as you want. Redecorating could take awhile."

"Thanks, sugar. But I'm going to check into one of those little specialty hotels on Massachusetts Avenue. You were darling to let me stay, but I want to protect both your privacy and mine. I'm usually out late at night, and that could be awkward. Besides, I don't want to cramp your style. In case that handsome ex-Marine makes a move one night, and you succumb to his charms."

I snickered over the phone. I heard the smile in Samantha's voice, and that made me feel good. "I don't think I'm 'succumbable' anymore. In fact, I doubt I ever was."

"Nonsense, sugar, you've just never had anybody who could really reach you. But I have a feeling he's the one."

Perceptive as ever. Samantha was definitely back and all her instincts were on alert. "Well, you may be right about that, Miss Thing. All the more reason to be on guard with Danny tonight. He's arriving today, and we're going out to dinner."

This time an exaggerated sigh came over the phone. "Lord, Molly, I don't know what I'm gonna do with you."

"Listen, you get that designer on the line,

and I'll get back to e-mails. Let me know which hotel you decide you're checking into. Oh, and let me know what your lawyer has to say now that the gossip is starting."

"I'll do that. Talk to you later, Molly. And thank you, again. For being there."

"Anytime, Miss Thing."

I clicked out of my e-mail inbox. Five o'clock and I'd cleared all the e-mails. Now I would have time to walk home and change for dinner with Danny tonight. I couldn't believe I was finishing early.

As I straightened the files on my desk, I remembered that I hadn't heard from Samantha since morning. I quickly found her number on my personal phone's directory, curious to know if her lawyer had convinced her to come clean about her evening companion the night Wilson killed himself.

She picked up after the second ring. "I knew that was you. Sorry I hadn't called. I've been on the phone all day with the people working on my house. It's a nightmare."

"Well, you can update me later. I'm more interested in what your lawyer told you. And please tell me you listened."

"Sugar, you know I *always* listen. I just don't follow instructions very well," she said in a light tone.

I let out an exasperated sigh and slapped some file folders down on my desk. "*Dammit*, Samantha! Stop being obstinate. You have to tell the police that man's name. If he's really a close friend, he'd want you to. None of us wants to see you hurt."

Samantha released a tired sigh. "Oh, I'm gonna be hurt no matter what happens. There's no way to avoid it. My lawyer said the police told him those photos were safely secured. But even if I believed them, the details of what's on the photos will slip out. You and I know that. This is Washington. Secrets aren't safe here. Someone always finds out. And if you're unlucky, a lot of people find out."

She was right, of course. Samantha and I had witnessed far too many scandals over the years, from the laughable to the lurid. Nothing was safe in Washington. *Nothing.* If it was worth something, then someone would find out. Nothing was sacred. And it sure wasn't safe.

That little worried feeling squeezed inside. "Samantha, please don't put yourself through this. Give the police his name. *Please.* I'm worried about you."

"I know you are and I appreciate it, sugar. But I have to be true to my principles. Now, you have a wonderful dinner with Danny, and tell that good man hello for me. I'll talk with you later. Bye, bye." Her phone clicked off one second before my office phone came to life. Peter calling.

"Don't worry. I've already called both offices, Peter. Now go have some dinner before you and the Senator attack that pile of financial research."

"Not enough time. I've already ordered pizza for the entire staff. The Senator is elbow deep in the research right now."

"I understand. Should I order a vat of coffee delivered or have you taken care of it?" I leaned back in my desk chair and checked my watch. Only five fifteen.

He chuckled. "Already taken care of."

My personal phone burst into life just then, "Brown Sugar" bouncing through the lazy summer late afternoon. Time to change the music.

"That's your private line, I can tell," Peter laughed. "Listen, I'll see you tomorrow."

"You bet." I clicked off and reached for the phone on the other side of my computer. Danny's name flashed on the screen, and my heart did its little skip.

"Hey, how're you doing? Have you landed yet? Or are you stuck waiting for a gate to open up?"

Danny's low voice chuckled and that made my pulse speed up to match Jagger's rhythm. "Nope. The only thing I'm waiting on right now is rush hour traffic. I'm on Interstate 66. Are you at home or still at the office?"

"Still at the office, but I'll be heading home as soon as I finish." I maneuvered my tail-less mouse, ready to log off.

"Okay, we'll rendezvous at your place. With luck, I'll get there before six."

"Sounds good. Oops, another call's coming in from Peter," I reached for my other phone again. "See you soon, Squad Leader."

"Roger that."

I rounded the corner from 29th onto P Street and hurried down the brick sidewalk. Peter's last phone call had necessitated four more follow-up calls, delaying my departure. Now, with any luck, D.C. traffic would slow Danny's progress as well, giving me time to change and . . . and . . .

Too late. I spotted Danny's sleek black sports car parked in my driveway, Danny leaning against the door. I sped up, careful to avoid the hidden hazards of Historic Georgetown sidewalks. Tripping over uneven bricks would send me into a less-than-graceful sprawl at the foot of my driveway. Not a good way to say hello.

I'd already glanced at my watch and knew it was past six o'clock, so I started my apologia as I headed up the driveway. "Sorry I'm late. Peter's call led to four more. I got away as fast as I could."

Danny pushed away from the car and approached. "No problem. I've only been here five minutes. Bruce and I've been getting reacquainted." He smiled that lazy smile I'd grown really fond of these last four months.

How any guy could look that relaxed after dealing with D.C. traffic for over an hour was beyond me. Relaxed and sexy, very sexy, with his sports coat, open collar, no tie. Casual — just enough.

"It'll only take me a minute, I promise —"

I didn't get to say more because Danny reached out and pulled me close, bringing his mouth to mine. His kiss was long and deep and warmer than warm. Waaaaay more. He broke it off just before my knees were about to give way.

When I caught my breath, I settled in for what I hoped was more. "Hello to you," I whispered. "I've missed that."

"Good. So have I." He grinned then kissed me lightly and pulled away. "Let's go to dinner. I'm starving."

"But I was going to change."

"You look great. C'mon," he said, encircling me with his arm as he escorted me to his car.

You gotta love a man that eloquent.

I licked the last drop of Gulab Jamun syrup from my spoon. Divine sugary delight. My glucose level was mounting by the minute, no doubt. Glancing about the sedate Indian restaurant in northwest Washington, I noticed several other diners had succumbed to the tempting desserts.

"Your friend Samantha is going to have to give up that guy's name," Danny said as he poured more chai tea into my cup. "Otherwise, she's going to loom large on the cops' radar screen."

"Don't I know it," I said, pushing away my licked-clean dessert dish and reaching for the chai. "Believe me, Danny, I've begged her to. So has her lawyer. He called her again this afternoon trying to convince her to tell the police. But Samantha swears she won't compromise this guy's privacy." I gave a disgusted, if unladylike, snort before enjoying the sweetened spicy beverage. The Indian waiter refilled Danny's coffee cup and smoothly whisked away the empty chai carafe in less than five seconds.

"Interesting priorities," Danny observed after sipping his coffee. "Samantha will jeopardize not only her own reputation but also her safety before she will compromise her companion's privacy." He gave a crooked smile. "I guess she has her own code of honor. I can respect that."

"Yes, she has. And loyalty is at the top of that list." I watched the silent, efficient waiter replace the newly filled chai carafe beside my cup. I toyed with having more. However, the heavy sugar dessert plus the sweet chai had already taken their toll. I felt the dreaded Sugar Sleep creeping through my veins. Time for coffee.

Danny looked at me and grinned. "It's time to take you home. I can tell you're getting sleepy." He signaled for the ever-observant waiter.

Damn. This man's perceptiveness was downright spooky. And unnerving. "Blame it on the dessert and chai. A double dose of sugar. And how could you tell anyway?" I teased. "I haven't yawned."

"By watching you. I've learned a lot of your signals these last four months," he said with a wink.

"That is seriously scary," I said in an

unguarded moment. It must have been the sugar.

All trace of a smile disappeared as Danny reached over and took my right hand. He brought it to his mouth for a warm kiss on my palm. "I know," Danny said, taking my hand in his. "But you don't have to be scared of me, Molly. I won't hurt you."

The Sugar Sleep fled my system in an instant. I was wide awake now. I looked into Danny's eyes, allowing him to see even deeper inside, and struggled for words that wouldn't come. The waiter came instead, so I managed to murmur, "I know."

Danny kissed my knuckles then released my hand to sign the check. "I've got an earlier-than-usual reveille tomorrow morning anyway. Have to be on I-95 by four thirty to avoid the rush hour traffic."

I made a face. "I'm not sure that's early enough. Where are you heading?"

"South. I've got an early morning appointment."

Now that I was wide awake, my naturally inquisitive nature reasserted itself. "South as in southern Virginia or farther south?" I probed playfully.

His lazy smile returned. "Southern Virginia."

"Hmmmmmm, I guess you could have an

early appointment at Smith Mountain Lake. I know fishermen who show up in the wee hours. Or, is there a larger body of water involved?"

"There's a lot of water nearby."

"I figured. And I'll bet there are a lot of really big boats floating nearby too." I caught his gaze and saw the laughter there.

"Not many boats, but a lot of ships."

"A sea voyage coming up?"

He shook his head as he came to stand behind my chair. "Nope. The closest I'll get to the water is looking at it through the window. Nothing but meetings back to back for a couple of days."

"Somehow I doubt you'll be bored," I challenged as I rose from my chair.

FIVE

I jerked awake. Loud guitar riffs bounced off my bedroom walls. *What the hell?* I squinted at the clock: 5:50. Who in the world would be calling me so early in the morning? Suddenly I thought of my elderly mother in her posh retirement home across the Potomac. I bolted from bed, snatching the phone before another Clapton guitar riff.

"Hello?" I rasped, my heart beating faster. Had she fallen? Was she ill? At nearly ninety years old, anything could happen.

Samantha's soft voice came over the phone. "Molly? I woke you up, I'm sorry. I . . . I just wanted to make sure I caught you before you went out for your morning run."

Relieved that some professional health-care provider wasn't on the other end of the line, I sat on the edge of the bed. "Samantha? What's the matter? You're not usually up until eight. Has something happened?"

"No, no, nothing's happened. I simply wanted to see if you'd please come over to my house for a few moments before you report in at your office. Late last night, I remembered I hadn't checked my surveillance video. I rarely check it. Usually the security company calls me if there's anything questionable. But I suddenly remembered and accessed it last night. And . . . and I saw something strange. I wanted you to come over and take a look. I'd like your opinion."

Surveillance video? "I never knew you had a security camera running. Where is it?"

"Right above the front door. It's concealed within one of the medallions. As I said, the security firm reviews each video. Quentin had already been cleared so his arrivals and departures were merely noted on the monthly summary. Sometimes I even forget to look at the summary. But last night I decided to take a look at the video myself, and I saw a man come to the door that night. The night Quentin died. Some man in a jacket and a hat. I couldn't see his face, but his jacket had some kind of logo or something on it. Maybe he was a repairman looking for a nearby address. My housekeeper tells me that people often ring the doorbell asking for directions."

"Hmmm, that is strange. Now you've made me curious."

"Good. I'd like you to take a look at the video and tell me what you think."

"All right. Give me a few minutes and I'll be there. Traffic shouldn't be too bad going in your direction this early. Coming back will be trickier."

"I promise I won't keep you, Molly. I simply want your opinion before I take this video to my lawyer. He can deliver it to the police."

"Better make a copy, just in case," I said, heading toward the shower.

"Already have."

I leaned closer to the large computer screen as Samantha advanced through the surveillance video. A man's image approached her front door, carrying a briefcase and talking on a cell phone.

"There's Quentin arriving," Samantha said. "You can see him put down his briefcase and then key in the entry code."

I observed the time at the upper right corner of the screen: 5:20. I watched Wilson bend over for his briefcase and reach out with his other hand for something else.

Then he disappeared inside the house.

"It looks like he picked up something. He was in the way, so I couldn't see what it was."

"Probably dropped his car keys," Samantha said as she fast-forwarded through the video. "Now, here's the guy walking up to the doorway: 5:52. See? Doesn't that look kind of like a repairman's hat and jacket?"

I observed a shorter, stocky man approach Samantha's front door; he paused for a moment then knocked. His hat did resemble some of the old-fashioned hats that service repair people used to wear. I peered at the back of his jacket as the man moved slightly side-to-side and started gesturing with his hands. I assumed he was talking to Wilson at that point.

"See? He's talking with Quent. Wait a minute . . . when he turns a little, you can glimpse a logo of some sort. There!"

I caught a brief glimpse of a blue-and-white rectangle on the back of the man's jacket.

"Yeah, you're right. But I can't tell what it is." The man pointed behind him toward the front yard, but the hat brim kept me from seeing his face. "He's pointing at something. I wonder what it is? Maybe he had a service truck or something in the driveway."

"Maybe or maybe he was simply asking for directions," Samantha said. "See . . . Quent comes out of the house then."

"Looks like he's pointing too. Well, kind of," I said, observing Wilson — jacket off, shirtsleeves rolled up — start to walk toward the front yard with the man and out of camera range.

"There they go. I figure Quent's giving the man directions. Samantha advanced the video forward. "Now, about five minutes pass, and Quent comes back, see?"

I watched Wilson return to the front door, pause, then glance over his shoulder briefly before re-entering the house. "I wonder what he was looking at?"

"Maybe the man was backing a truck out of the driveway," Samantha suggested as she fast-forwarded the video again. "But now, here comes the part I find really puzzling. Over an hour has passed. And look who shows up again."

I checked the video time again and it read 7:23. To my surprise, the same stocky guy in hat and jacket approached the door again and knocked. "Well, well, Mister Repairman. Wonder why he came back?"

"That's what puzzles me, as well as this. Watch."

The repairman stood on the front stoop, shifting from one foot to the other, obviously waiting. Then, he knocked on the door again, longer this time.

"I wonder why Wilson hasn't come to the door yet?" I wondered out loud.

"Yes, I thought that strange too. Here he comes now. See . . . the door opens and Quent leans out. The repairman is telling him something, see?"

The repairman was clearly explaining something, because he was gesturing even more and pointed again toward the front yard. Or, maybe the driveway. "You know, Samantha, I'll bet that guy had car or truck problems and was trying to fix it. Maybe that's why he came back."

"I'm thinking that's what it is, too, and look at Quent. He's on the phone now; see it pressed to his ear? And he's upset. Really upset. I can tell from the way he's waving his arm. That's what he does when he's talking on the phone and getting agitated. That's probably Quent's wife calling him about the photos. His cell phone log showed her call coming in a little after seven." Samantha shook her head. "Poor Quentin. Look at him."

Wilson had stepped onto the front stoop and was animatedly gesturing to the repair guy, pointing toward the front yard, arm waving, phone still pressed to his ear. After a moment, Wilson went back inside the house, and the repair guy walked out of camera range toward the front yard — or the driveway.

"You know, I think that's it, Samantha. He's got truck or car trouble, and maybe he's stuck in the driveway. Maybe that's the reason Wilson's so mad. He wants to leave, but he can't. What do you think?"

She shrugged. "That's as good an explanation as any. That's got to be why the repairman reappeared." She fast-forwarded through the video again. "He doesn't appear again, so whatever repair problems he had were obviously fixed."

I watched the video time stamp run through the hours — ten o'clock, eleven o'clock, midnight, one o'clock. "And Quentin doesn't reappear either."

"No, he doesn't . . . poor thing," Samantha said sadly. "That phone call from his wife was the last one. After that, nothing." Samantha sat back in her chair and stared at the screen. "I called Natasha Jorgensen yesterday. I used the number I'd copied from his cell phone log, betting it would be hers. Quentin never let on, but I'm betting she knew about our relationship. Natasha needed to know where Quent was all the time. It would have been hard to explain our weekend getaways otherwise."

"Why'd you call her?"

Samantha turned to me, her deep blue gaze direct. "I wanted to know if she'd seen any signs of depression or panic the last day he was alive. Quent had gone to his office for a staff meeting, so Natasha and the rest of the staff would have been there. If Quentin was beginning to slide into some suicidal depression, surely there would have been a sign . . . something that Natasha would have picked up on. I mean, she was his closest aide."

"What did Natasha say? Did he seem depressed to her?"

"No, just the opposite. She said Quentin appeared hyper that Saturday at the office, more agitated than usual. That's understandable, given the surprise package we both received that morning. I told her that I simply couldn't believe Quentin deliberately took too many pills. I still can't. Natasha agreed with me. She said she was guilt-ridden, wondering if there was something she could have picked up on or seen. Maybe she could have stopped him."

"Natasha couldn't have done anything," I interjected. "I'm thinking that Quentin didn't plan on doing it, but he may have been so distraught after his wife's phone call that he wasn't paying attention. Natasha said he was already hyper when he was at the office. And you said he was frantic when he called you. If anything pushed Quentin over the edge, it would have been his wife's phone call. Maybe she told him she was filing for divorce immediately. That could have done it. You said he would be finished in Ohio if she went after him."

"That's true. Maybe he'd already taken some pills before her call and then took even more afterwards." Samantha stared out into the room. "It would be so much easier to bear if it was accidental."

"It must have been. After all, he was drinking the Guinness, and alcohol magnifies the effects and makes it worse. Then that repair guy came to the door again in the middle of his wife's phone call. That must have really set Quentin off."

She shook her head. "Poor Quentin. He was probably so panicked after her call he didn't know what he was doing. I bet that's why the coffee table had pills scattered all around, some opened and spilling out. Police told my lawyer they even found pills dissolved in the bottle of Guinness."

"That's strange."

"I thought so too. He probably wasn't thinking at all by that time. Poor Quentin," she repeated and continued to fast-forward though the early morning hours of the video, slowing down when the time clock read 6:20. At precisely 6:33, Samantha appeared at the front door, pausing to key in her code, and entered. "And there I am," she said in a soft voice. She stopped advancing the video. "And I don't leave. The next people to appear at the door are the Fairfax County Police." She released the tail-less mouse and sank back in her desk chair.

I stared at the lingering video screen shot showing Samantha's empty front porch. "You'll take this video to your lawyer this morning, I trust."

"Oh, yes. I left a message on his personal voice mail telling him that I'd drop by with the video." She reached for the mouse again and began to reverse the video. "I'll make sure to show him the exact same sections we've looked at and see what his reaction is."

I watched the images go backwards. "Plus, he can show the delivery man to the police. That way, you stay out of it."

"My thoughts exactly."

I reached for my forgotten cup of coffee. Half-full and stone-cold now. I took a sip anyway. Glancing toward the screen, I noticed a quick image flash by. It looked like a man. "Wait a minute." I pointed to the screen. "I just saw another guy on your porch. Go forward again."

"Probably some delivery man. They come by regularly," she said as the images moved forward, more slowly this time.

"Stop right there at 4:15. Let it play," I said and pointed at the screen again as the image of a man appeared, walking up to Samantha's front door. There was something in his hand. "See, he's carrying something. It looks like a mailing envelope. Same color."

Samantha peered at the screen. "Yeah, it does."

The man looked around the front porch, looked behind him, then glanced above the front door. He paused long enough to stare right into Samantha's surveillance camera.

"That's a young guy," I said. "And he's not wearing a uniform, just street clothes. He doesn't look like a delivery man."

Samantha's eyes narrowed. "No, he doesn't."

The young guy leaned over and placed the mailing envelope beside the front door, then glanced around again before he walked away — out of camera range.

I'd also noticed something else. "He didn't ring the doorbell, Samantha, and he didn't knock. Are you sure you didn't ask someone to drop something off at your house?"

"No, I didn't. But I know who did. *Dammit!*"

Her sudden anger took me by surprise. "Who?"

"Quentin! That guy has to be the one who supplied Quent with his pills. He said he used some young staffer who worked at the Congressional Research Service. His uncle's an internist and filled the prescriptions. Quent said the guy delivered them to his house, and Quent paid him in cash."

"*What!* I cannot believe Wilson would take such a risk. That was definitely not smart."

"I know, I know." She shook her head. "I told Quent the same thing, but he insisted he needed the pills."

"Wouldn't his doctor supply him with sleeping pills?"

Samantha released a long sigh. "It was more than that. Quentin also took Vicodin occasionally, and his doctor would only prescribe a little of that."

I closed my eyes. I had heard this story before. Too many times. Opiate-based painkillers. Blessed relief from pain for some. A dangerous path for others.

"Oh, God . . . how often did he take them?"

"He'd use Vicodin sometimes when he was really having problems sleeping. Certainly not all the time. At least not when he was with me. He kept the pills in his briefcase, so who knows?" She stared at the screen sadly. "He told me he tried to be careful."

I watched as Samantha reversed the video once more. Checking my watch, I computed how long it would take me to get to the office. It was 7:30 now, but I'd be right in the midst of rush hour traffic on Chain Bridge Road. Even weaving around residential streets, I'd still be stuck. Might as well just get onto the G.W. Parkway and fight my way across Key Bridge with everyone else. It didn't matter where you started in Virginia, if you were headed to Washington, the Potomac River had to be crossed.

"You'd better go, Molly. I'm afraid you're gonna get stuck in that mess." Samantha pushed away from her desk.

"Yeah, I'd better join the herd." I drained the rest of the yucky coffee and followed Samantha out of the library.

"Thanks again for coming over so early. I appreciated getting your reaction to that video, especially the last part." She grimaced.

"You know you can count on me, Samantha," I said as I slipped my purse over my shoulder. "And let me know what your lawyer says. Keep me posted, okay?"

"Count on it, Molly," she said with a smile. It was the first smile I'd seen from her that morning.

I sipped the delicate Pinot Noir and savored its lush yet subtle flavors as I stood at the edge of Senator Russell's elegant living room, watching tonight's guests mingle. The wine merchants that my cousins Nan and Deb had personally recommended had not disappointed. The senator's wine list had been upgraded without making a huge dent in the entertaining budget. That made me very happy since I was in charge of all of the senator's household and entertaining expenses.

Tonight's reception was smaller than most of the Senator's earlier ones. This guest list focused solely on Senator Russell's colleagues on his other Senate committee, Energy and Natural Resources. Several members were from Western states. As was my usual game-day plan, I welcomed arriving guests and shepherded them toward the caterer's temptations, as well as the bartender's.

The serving staff from the private firm that the senator employed for entertaining were experienced with all manner of political functions and moved smoothly and efficiently throughout any group, large or small. Since the senator had been entertaining the entire Congress over the last four months I'd been working for him, I'd become well-acquainted with all of the staff of Preferred Professionals. We were battlefield comrades together. Nothing kept you on your toes like a room full of demanding politicians and their egos.

July's heat had kept all but a handful of guests inside the living room in the air-conditioned cool. Old pro Aggie and graduate student Ryan moved smoothly through the clusters of Senators, spouses, and chief staffers offering tempting appetizers and replenishing drinks. Talking made most people thirsty. Since politicians talked more than most people — a lot more — they were thirstier. Hence, Aggie worked a nonstop route between the bar and the guests. Each replenished tray was emptied quickly. Bartender Bud was an efficient machine, fast and smooth. Filling drink orders, pouring wines, and mild non-alcoholic choices for those who wanted to keep their wits about them and their tongues in check. The Senate chamber was filled with very powerful people. Some of them were in this room tonight, I observed. One careless remark could damage an up-and-coming staffer's career. I'd seen that happen more times than I cared to remember.

I spotted Aggie return from supplying the handful of sun-worshippers on the patio and then head to the bar yet again. Ryan walked my way with his empty tray. "Looks like the caterer's peppered beef was a success. You've been running back and forth to the kitchen faster than normal," I said as Ryan approached.

"Ohhhh, yeah. They went through those peppered beef canapés fast. Good thing the caterer brought more of the brie and pastry and the curried chicken. Man, this is one hungry group," Ryan said with a smile. His smile made him look even younger, much younger than his thirty-three years.

"Let's keep them happy. Feed them and water them well is my motto," I joked as we walked down the side hallway toward the kitchen. Curiosity suddenly pushed forward and I couldn't help asking. "I imagine there's a lot of talk about Congressman Wilson's death going around."

"Oh, yeah, I've heard it mentioned several times. That's such a shame too. He seemed to be a really sharp guy. I heard him interviewed on a news show a few months ago." Ryan paused outside the doorway to the kitchen. I could see the catering staff scurrying around in their seemingly frantic, but-always-in-control routines. "Today's news reports said he died from an accidental overdose of sleeping pills. That is so sad. And such a waste too."

"I agree, Ryan. We've lost a lot of good and talented people this year. We really can't afford to lose any more." My niece Karen's face flashed through my mind. Too young to die so young or so violently. Chasing away gruesome memories, I ventured into the caterers' domain. "Do we have any coffee set up yet?" I asked Ryan. "I'm about to switch poisons."

"Sure, Molly. Want me to get you a cup?"

"That's okay, just point me in the right direction." I scanned the command center where caterers were giving orders. I deliberately stayed out of their way. Artists at Work.

"Coffee's over there," Caterer Rosen called out, pointing to a side counter. "You can come in, Molly. We won't bite."

"It's not you I'm worried about," I said, heading for the tall urns. The coffee lobe of my brain was still lulled by the rich wine. Time to wake it up. "I don't want to step in someone's way as they're dashing about. A soufflé might fall, or worse, a whole tray of yummy things." I noticed a tray with crab delicacies on another counter as I filled a coffee cup. "Actually I don't trust myself to be around all your great food. I'll lose control and start eating."

"That's music to our ears, Molly," Caterer Marian said with a wide smile. She was the older of the successful twosome.

"Go ahead, have one," Ryan tempted me, his tray already filled with the spinach-and-cheese-filled phyllo pastries.

I can only resist so much, so I snatched one and popped it into my mouth, letting those delicious and fattening flavors delight. "Too delicious. I'm out of here before I lose control," I sped for the doorway, following Ryan, as the catering staff's laughter drifted behind me.

A deep drink of coffee chased away the rich flavors and the wine's mellowing effects. Now I'd be sure to stay sharp. I didn't want to miss any comments about Quentin Wilson's death. Aggie was heading my way, a lone glass of red wine on her tray.

"I saved a Pinot Noir for you, Molly, but I see you've already switched to coffee," she said with her familiar smile.

"Thanks anyway, Aggie. You can give it to one of those sunbathers outside."

"Actually they've been ordering iced drinks, no surprise," Aggie started toward the bar.

"I'll bet the gossip hounds are in full bay with the Quentin Wilson news," I walked with her.

"Oh, yes." Aggie's smile disappeared. "I've overheard a lot of people remarking about it. It's a real shame."

"Have you heard anyone speculating about where Wilson died?" I probed. "The paper mentioned a Northern Virginia residence."

Aggie stopped and looked at me, her gaze direct. "Why are you asking?"

I noticed she didn't answer my question, but I wasn't surprised. I was convinced she'd been a spook in her earlier years. Whether she was still reporting to someone, only Aggie knew. She'd been working these Washington parties for over thirty years, always hovering near the movers and shakers.

I met Aggie's direct gaze and decided on total honesty. "I figure it's simply a matter of time before the gossip turns nasty. Wilson was found at the home of my oldest and dearest friend. She was the one who walked in and found him dead Sunday morning. I'm the only one she called after the police left."

Aggie's gray eyes widened quickly, and I could see the puzzle pieces being sorted as she digested the information. "Are we talking about the late Senator Calhoun's widow?"

"We are, indeed. She and Congressman Wilson were . . . close friends," I hedged. "So I'm concerned that the gossip will turn vicious once word spreads. I'd appreciate it if you'd tell me if you overhear any particularly ugly rumors. That way, I can give her a warning."

Aggie's little smile returned. "I'd be glad to, Molly. I remember you and your friend attending some of your father's parties years ago. You two made quite a pair. I also used to work Senator Calhoun's parties whenever I could."

Why was I not surprised? Samantha's husband had been one of the most powerful men in the Senate while he was alive. Naturally, Aggie would have been at his parties, listening and learning. Wherever there was liquor, lips as well as inhibitions were loosened. Information spilled out as easily as wine from a glass.

"Thanks, Aggie. I'm sure you've paid attention over the last few years to my friend's rather . . . ah, rebellious lifestyle. I'm afraid she's made a few enemies, and that's always dangerous in this town. So, I'm trying to look out for her however I can."

"I understand. And I'll keep an ear out. For the record, I did hear part of a conversation that mentioned her name along with Congressman Wilson."

I grimaced. "I knew it would start. Was that the only one?"

Aggie shook her head as she edged away. "No, there were two other couples talking about it, I'm sorry to say. Take care, Molly, and give my regards to your friend." Aggie scurried off to the bar.

Damn. It had started already. Needless to say, tonight's reception provided the perfect opportunity to exchange gossip. I glanced about the living room again. Political types, elected or otherwise, clustered together talking, laughing, drinking, finger waving, arguing, eating. Senator Russell was near the fireplace, with the senior senator from Utah. Senator Russell threw back his head and let out his trademark basso roar of laughter. It was all I could do to hear him over the gossip's rising buzz. Louder than the cicadas in the trees outside.

"Did you talk to that staffer, Levitz, yet?"

Larry Fillmore sped past the Capitol Reflecting Pool, cell phone pressed to his ear. Six forty-five, and the sun was still blazing down. *Damn Washington summers.* Larry could tell Spencer wanted to talk, but he wasn't about to stand near the Capitol with all the tourists and sweat.

"Yeah, this afternoon. I showed up in his office at the Rayburn building, purportedly with some research questions from Congressman Jackson. Then I asked him to walk me out. Told him I had a message for him. He probably thought I was going to place an order."

"How was this staffer pulling it off? He's working right in the middle of Capitol Hill, for God's sake."

"His uncle's an internist in Bethesda and he fills the prescription orders that Levitz phones in. Levitz then picks them up from a dummy office every evening and makes deliveries. Everyone pays cash."

"Pretty sweet little system they had going. Helping out the hyper politicians and staffers who want more drugs than their doctors give them. And no records."

"You got it. Anyway, that's when I came on like the older and wiser Capitol Hill staffer. Big brother, like. Told him that I'd heard about his delivery business on the side, then added he might want to keep a low profile now that Wilson was dead from an overdose that *he* delivered."

"You probably scared the crap out of him when you said that. What'd he do?"

"Turned white as a sheet," Larry smirked as he glanced over both shoulders before crossing Jefferson Drive. Trees bordering the Mall up ahead beckoned. Shade was almost within reach. "Then I told him he might want to think about leaving town until the Wilson death was put to bed completely. I mean, if I could find out about his delivery business, the cops sure as hell could. Too many people knew. He started shaking like a leaf."

Spencer's deep chuckle sounded over the phone despite the traffic noise. "I'll bet."

"That's when I gave him that disposable cell phone's number. I told him to call me if he needed help because I knew people who could provide some cover. I then added that I liked his ambitious spirit and didn't want to see him get dragged down by Quentin Wilson's problems. Wilson had been screwing around on his wife for a long time.

She probably found out and filed for divorce. His wife was bankrolling Wilson's career. So, he'd be Ohio roadkill from now on. No surprise the guy swallowed those pills."

Spencer laughed low in his throat. "Damn, that's good. You've almost got me believing it."

"Yeah, well it may sound like a worn-out cliché, but that's why it's believable . . . *hey! Watch it!*" Larry jumped out of the way as several tourists on large-wheeled touring vehicles passed right in front of him. *"Son of a bitch!"* he muttered into the phone.

"What the hell happened?"

"Damn tourists nearly ran into me on those ridiculous rolling things! Tourists on wheels. They're a damn pedestrian hazard!" Larry scowled as he walked. Now that he was on the Mall's well-trod ground, he'd be plagued by even more tourists, kids dripping ice cream cones, screaming babies.

"Don't be so hard on them. They bring in a ton of cash," Spencer joked.

"Pain in the ass, if you ask me," Larry said as he reached the tall trees' shade at last. He could feel a sunburn starting already on his rarely seen-the-sun skin. He spied an empty bench and sat before a group of sticky-fingered kids claimed it.

"Hey, it's July. High Season. They'll start heading home third week in August. Get the kids into school, back into jobs and routines. You know, family life. Oh . . . that's right. You didn't have any kids so you don't know about all that."

Larry could hear the jibe in Spencer's voice. "You're right. Snotty-nosed little urchins crawling on my lap never appealed to me."

Spencer laughed softly. "You're all brain and no heart, Larry. Just what we need. That reminds me, we may need some gossip-media help keeping the Wilson story on script. So get your contacts ready."

"They're always ready," Larry said, deliberately sending a big smile to the family group walking the Mall path in front of him.

Six

Wednesday

"Hey, Casey!" I called as I spotted the security guard leaving the Russell kitchen, coffee mug in hand. "Do you have a minute?"

"Sure Molly. What's up?" he said as we met in the middle of the hallway.

I glanced toward the open doorway leading to the garden. "I wanted to run something by you. Why don't we step outside for a second. It's such a glorious morning."

Casey's weathered face crinkled into a smile. "In other words, you need privacy to ask your question. Sure. Let's take some fresh air before the humidity rises."

"Boy, I must need to work on my signals because you're starting to see right through me," I joked as we headed through the French doors leading outside.

The well-manicured Russell garden was green and lush, thanks to the gardening crew's copious watering and Washington's occasional summer thunderstorm. The rose bushes were laden with blossoms and all sizes of blooms — crimson reds, snowflake whites, buttery yellows, and soft hues of lavender and pink. Other flowering shrubs abounded as did low-level border plants. I paused beside a gardenia bush with pearl white blooms, wide open. A delicate scent floated upward on the morning's humid air, teasing my nostrils. Edging the entire squared garden were tall, thick boxwood hedges. Green screens of privacy. Their distinctive scent bringing back memories of leisurely strolls through so many of Virginia's historic gardens.

"Reading people is part of my job, Molly," Casey said, following me down the flagstone path. "What's on your mind?"

I paused for a second, deciding how best to broach the subject. "I'm sure you've heard me speak of my old friend, Samantha Calhoun. Senator Beauregard Calhoun's widow."

"Yes, I recall your mentioning her. The two of you grew up together in Washington, I believe."

"Yes, we did, and we tried to stay out of trouble in those days. The advice given to us was 'Don't do anything you wouldn't want printed on the front page of the *Washington Post.*' " I gave in to the enticing scent below and leaned over to sniff a deep crimson rose's perfume.

Casey chuckled. "Words to live by, I'd say. Was that your father's advice?"

"Actually it was Eleanor MacKenzie's advice. She sort of watched over Samantha and me years ago, helping us stay out of trouble. We used to call her the Queen Mother."

This time Casey laughed out loud. "I can see Mrs. MacKenzie in that role. She's a special lady even now. But why are we out here in the garden reminiscing, Molly?"

I turned and looked into Casey's intent dark gaze. "Because I'm afraid my friend Samantha is involved in something that could become fodder for lesser papers than the *Post.* Congressman Wilson chose to end his life at Samantha's home while she was out for the evening. She told me she returned early Sunday morning and found him dead on her sofa."

Surprise flashed briefly through his eyes. "Hmmm. That's not good."

"Tell me about it. Samantha and Wilson had been having an affair since the beginning of this year. And you know how Washington is. You can never keep those things secret for long. That's why I'm telling you, Casey. I know I can trust your discretion, but I wanted to ask if you'd overheard any gossip the other evening. About Samantha and Wilson, that is. I've already asked Aggie and Ryan. They heard bits and pieces."

Casey examined his coffee mug. "As a matter of fact, I did. Of course, the comments were more innuendo and speculation, though. But one woman did mention she was convinced the Northern Virginia home mentioned in the newspaper was Samantha Calhoun's. So, I'm afraid the gossip is spreading."

"*Damn.* Samantha and Wilson were ending their affair that very day. That's why Wilson was at Samantha's house that evening. He'd returned to gather some personal belongings. Why he chose to end his life there, we don't know. But Samantha called the police as soon as she found him."

"Where was she when it happened? Did she tell you?"

"All she's said was that she was with an old friend and confidant in Washington." I let my annoyed expression finish the sentence.

Casey looked over the rose bushes. "That's not good, either. She needs to establish her whereabouts for that evening. If she was still in the house while Wilson was there, well . . . it raises questions and invites speculation. You know that."

"Yes, I do," I said, exhaling an exasperated breath. "Believe me, I've been trying to convince her and so has her lawyer. Police are bound to become suspicious of her refusal to answer. That's where I'd like to ask you a favor, Casey."

He arched one of his bushy brows. "If you're asking me to find out what the Fairfax County Police will do, I'm afraid I can't help you much. Most of my connections are here in D.C. But I do have an old friend from the Marines in the Fairfax Department, so I could ask him to update me if he learns anything. Sounds like this death is being handled as a suicide, so there shouldn't be anything unusual. Of course, Ms. Calhoun still needs to inform the police where she was that night so there won't be any problems."

"Believe me, I'm working on her." I paused for a second, debating what I was about to say next. "There is one more thing."

Casey leveled his gaze on me. "And what would that be?"

"Yesterday morning, Samantha called me to her place early to see a video her surveillance camera recorded. The camera is directly over her front door, so it shows everyone who comes and leaves."

"Did you know she had a surveillance system?"

"I knew she had a very reputable security company taking care of her properties, but I didn't know about the camera over the front door. The video showed Wilson entering the house that evening, then later on, it shows some guy who looked like a repairman come to the door. Wilson went outside with him, then returned to the house. We figured the guy had car or truck trouble. Anyway, no one comes in or leaves the house for the rest of the evening. Samantha arrived about six thirty a.m. But something else caught my attention before Wilson even arrived that evening."

"What was that?"

"It was something I noticed when Samantha was reversing the video. A guy showed up in the late afternoon. A young guy. Looked to be in his late twenties. Blond, short hair, kind of spiked. Casually dressed but nice. He was carrying some kind of envelope. Samantha said people stop by frequently, asking her housekeeper for directions. But I watched and he never rang the doorbell or knocked. Instead, he just left the envelope beside the door. But he looked all around first, then looked straight up into the camera."

I noticed that Casey's gaze had sharpened on me. "Did Samantha recognize him?"

"No, but she did get upset. When I asked if she'd ordered something to be delivered, she said no, but she knew who did."

"Who?"

"Quentin Wilson. Apparently he used some Hill staffer with doctor connections to supply him with prescription sleeping pills and painkillers." I watched Casey's eyes widen. "Samantha said Wilson took Vicodin whenever he was really agitated and the sleeping pills weren't enough."

"Did Wilson ever tell Samantha the guy's name?"

"No, but she remembered Wilson said the guy worked at the Congressional Research Service."

Casey stared out across the garden for a long minute. "And Ms. Calhoun told you about that video yesterday, which was Monday. That was a whole day after she discovered Wilson dead in her home. Did Ms. Calhoun tell the police about the video when they came to the house Sunday morning?"

"She told me she just remembered it

yesterday. But she did say she called her lawyer. He was supposed to deliver the video to the police yesterday afternoon. And I can tell what you're thinking. This looks bad."

"It sure does. Waiting more than a day to remember you have a surveillance camera is kind of hard to explain, especially when it contains video that would help the investigation. Considering she's also refused to say where she was that night, well . . . you can imagine how that looks to police."

"Not good, I know." I stared off into the rose bushes once more.

"Look, Molly, I'll call my friend and see what he's heard about the investigation into Wilson's death. It could be routine suicide follow-up. But I'll be sure to tell him this information you've discovered."

"Well, I thought police should know about this guy. Otherwise they might see the video and think he's someone delivering an order. Meanwhile, I'll work on Samantha."

I heard Casey's cell phone's ringtone cut through the familiar cicada background drone, and I backed away as he pulled out his phone. "I'll talk to you later," he said quickly before answering.

I quickly retreated up the steps, summer morning heat rising around me. I could feel the dampness on my skin already. Expense spreadsheets were waiting for me in my office: Russell expenses and Brewster's rental properties. The thickening humidity chased me inside and I closed the French doors behind me, escaping into the air-conditioned cool. Maybe I'd make that next cup of morning coffee iced.

I tabbed through the spreadsheet columns, entering expenses as the string quartet played softly from the speakers I'd set up on the bookcase behind me. A Bach sonata. Nothing like Bach to order the mind. Brewster's several rental properties were all occupied and yielding a profit after expenses. Always good news for property investors.

Clapton's guitar riffs momentarily overpowered Bach's brilliant counterpoint. Brilliance in another form. I grabbed my personal phone and recognized my cousin Nan's name and number flashing.

"Hey, how are you? Are we still on for this Saturday evening? What can I bring?" I asked as I leaned back in the contoured chair.

"Yes, we are, and food is all taken care of," Nan said, her voice sounded like she was driving. "But we can always use more wine. There'll be twelve or so, depending if our neighbors can make it."

"You got it. Let me know if you need anything else."

"By the way, I was just at a client's home discussing the dinner Deb and I are arranging for her, and her television was on in the kitchen. A morning news show was interviewing Congressman Wilson's widow. She's in town to arrange a memorial service for her husband before his burial in Ohio, but she suddenly started talking about her husband's death and insisting it wasn't a suicide, and how she wants it investigated, and on and on like that."

"*What!* When was this? Which channel?"

"I don't know because we weren't in the kitchen long enough to find out. Plus, I was trying to listen to the reporter with one ear and my client with the other. But it was about ten o'clock or so. Wilson's widow also made some reference to her husband's 'companion' for the evening, as she put it. That's not good. I wondered how Samantha's reacting."

That definitely wasn't good news. Now, not just Washington insiders but the general public would start to wonder about Wilson's companion and ask questions. I felt a little muscle squeeze inside, realizing Samantha's fifteen minutes of notoriety were about to begin. I had a sinking feeling that it would last a lot longer than fifteen minutes.

"I'll call her now and find out. *Damn.* What's up with that Wilson woman? Widows are supposed to be grieving or sorrowful or at least quiet. Hell, I barely opened my mouth after Dave's suicide, even with all those flash bulbs popping in my face."

Old memories suddenly reappeared before my eyes, sharp and startling. Me, standing outside our Georgetown rowhouse, my arms around my two little girls, trying to weave a path to a waiting limousine. Silently shepherding my tearful children safely through the press gauntlet. *Speak?* I was still shell-shocked. Walking into that grisly scene, finding my young husband lying in a pool of his own blood and gore. Half of his head blown away. Gun still in his hand. *How could I speak. What could I say?* I still didn't understand. Not then, not now. Forgiveness, grudging and incomplete, had been slow in coming.

"Yeah, I thought it was kind of strange too. That's why I called. And don't worry. Deb and I aren't opening our mouths."

"Thanks, Nan. I know I can trust you two."

"That's pretty good for Washington,"

Nan's tone turned lighter. "If you have two or three people you can trust in this city, that's doing pretty good. Talk to you later, I've got a call coming in."

"See you Saturday." I clicked off my cell and was about to call Samantha, then decided I'd take another stroll in the gardens outside. This conversation definitely required privacy. Besides, there was a gazebo in a garden corner that should have captured the afternoon shade by now.

I took my mug of iced coffee and headed down the hallway once more. The Russell mansion had settled into early afternoon quiet. There was no entertaining scheduled for this evening, so no caterers were bustling about the kitchen or setting up in the living and dining rooms. My high heels echoed in the tall-ceilinged rooms and hallway as I walked.

The heavy summer heat hit me in the face the moment I opened the glass door leading outside. I'd breached the air-conditioned cocoon. Stepping into the blazing sunshine's glare, I pressed Samantha's number on my phone and sped toward the gazebo, squinting. *Why hadn't I brought my sunglasses?*

Samantha answered on the third ring as I reached the gazebo's hot shade. The wooden panels fairly radiated with the sun's heat. I started to sit but jumped up the moment my rear end encountered the super-heated wood. "Hey, how're you doing?" I asked.

"Surviving," Samantha's drawl drew out the word. "Trying to keep my head down and stay out of sight, if you know what I mean."

I did. "I figure you've heard about the Widow Wilson's television interview. Nan just called me about it. I missed it."

"Ohhhhh, yes. I had several calls alerting me so I was able to tune in. She definitely lives up to Quentin's description of her, I'll say that."

"Apparently she insisted Wilson's death wasn't a suicide. What's up with that?"

"I have no idea. But I suspect we'll all find out shortly. I sense this woman has found she likes the spotlight and attention. I could just see it radiating off her. I mean, you and I have been around a long time, girl. Some people use tragic events to advance themselves. I recognized those signals coming off her. Big time."

"Unfortunately, I know what you mean. Let's hope she revels in her late husband's reflected spotlight and then heads home."

"Don't count on it. My sources tell me the Widow Wilson has been conferring with Ohio politicians. Word is she's lobbying to be appointed to fill Quentin's seat until the next election. Given how much Quent said she'd donated to the Governor's last campaign, I'd say she is a shoo-in. She must be, because my mice also said Quent's chief-of-staff Natasha Jorgensen has already left for Congresswoman Chertoff's office."

I pictured the dynamic congresswoman from Iowa. "Well, that was a smart move on Natasha's part. Sally Chertoff is sharper than most. She'll go far, I predict. And her staff will rise with her."

"Sally will be lucky to have Natasha. She's super smart and has great instincts. She was Quent's right arm."

"Then she'll be better off in Chertoff's office. Listen, Nan said the Widow Wilson also made some reference in that interview about her husband's evening companion. I don't like the sound of that."

Samantha made a genteel snort. "Nor do I. But, I'm bracing myself for more. You and I were guessing that she ordered those photos and had copies, so it looks like we were right. I have no idea how much this woman knows about me, but I have the feeling I'm about to find out."

"Dear God . . ."

"Oh, yeah," Samantha sighed wearily. "And if she's mad enough to turn vindictive, then it will get ugly. Quentin broke her cardinal rule. Keep it private."

"Well, at least the photos have been kept out of the papers," I said, trying to find something reassuring to say.

"So far. And pray that it stays that way. Like I said before, the police assured my lawyer that the photos were secured and sealed in their files. God, I hope so." Her voice grew softer.

I could feel Samantha's vulnerability come over the phone, and I responded automatically. "Listen, Samantha, I'm coming over tonight. I know you're staying out of the public eye right now, but you also need someone to talk to who isn't on the other end of a phone line. And don't argue with me. I'll run home and pack a bag and come over as soon as traffic allows."

"Aren't you and Danny going somewhere this evening? I don't want to interrupt anything."

I could hear the smile in her voice, and that made me feel better. "Nothing to interrupt. Danny's still down south in Virginia, consulting. Apparently some additional meetings were scheduled. Then he's got a trip to the West Coast scheduled as soon as he returns. So he'll be gone for a while."

"Well, that's sweet of you to come over,

Molly. I . . . I appreciate it."

I heard the telltale beep that signaled she had another call coming in on her line. "It's the least I can do, Miss Thing."

"My lawyer is ringing. Talk to you tonight."

"Later," I said, hearing her click off. Mentally running through my schedule, I rearranged some errands I'd planned for tonight. Considering I had to return home to pack an overnight bag, that would allow the worst of the traffic to move over the bridge and up the G.W. Parkway to McLean. Another half hour would really help. Hmmmmmm, maybe I could pass that time checking the news channels. With luck, I could catch a replay of the Widow Wilson's interview on the evening news. I wanted to see her in action.

SEVEN

Wednesday evening

"Did you see those two interviews on the news?" Raymond asked. "One this morning and another a few minutes ago."

"Yes, I saw them both." Spencer's exasperated sigh sounded over the phone. "*Damn.* I have to admit I didn't see this coming. Who would have thought Wilson's widow would come to Washington and raise a stink. She's a grieving widow, for God's sake!"

Raymond stood beside his office window. The turn-of-the-century rowhouses across the street were being demolished for new buildings. Probably another high-rise condo to block out his view. He sipped his creamy coffee. Double cream to coat his ragged throat. He'd said to hell with cholesterol years ago. Calories be damned as well. "It's a tabloid TV world, Spencer. Everybody wants their fifteen minutes of fame."

Spencer snorted. "Fame, my ass. I've been

asking around ever since this morning's interview and it seems Sylvia Wilson has ambitions of her own. She wants to take over her husband's Ohio seat. And she's prepared to call in her markers to do it. Her family's money helped the governor get elected twice, so he owes her big time."

"Sounds like she's a natural for Washington already," Raymond observed, watching a crane lift a metal beam from the skeletal remains of the building across the way. "I'm sure the others won't be too happy hearing all this extra publicity. Would you like me to run a deeper check on Sylvia Wilson?"

"Actually sources are already coming out of the woodwork. It seems Sylvia is a grade-A bitch and has run roughshod over her husband's congressional staffers these last few years. So they're anxious to tell everything they know about Congressman and Mrs. Wilson. And they know a *lot.*" Spencer's good-natured chuckle sounded once more. "Larry Fillmore is taking extensive notes."

"I'll bet. Well, let me know when you need additional services," Raymond said, settling back into his desk chair, his desk spread with papers and books.

"Absolutely. Meanwhile, relax and enjoy the melodrama. The Widow Wilson may not know it yet, but she's given us the perfect way to counter any suspicions about her husband's suicide. With the sleaze media's help, of course. Watch for it."

"Welcome to Washington politics, Widow Wilson," Raymond laughed, aggravating that cough, despite the cream.

I rang Samantha's doorbell and instinctively glanced up toward the carved floral medallion above the two double doors. Unable to resist, I smiled and waved in the general direction of the hidden camera.

"Come on in, sugar," Samantha said as she opened the door. "I've got your Cosmo chilling even as we speak."

Music to my ears. "Now, that's the kind of welcome a girl appreciates. Especially after evening traffic." I set my purse and travel bag on a nearby table. "First, let me give you a hug. You need one."

"You are so right," she said, squeezing me as we hugged. "Thanks so much for coming over tonight. I appreciate it more than you know. Especially after watching the latest news."

I followed Samantha into her huge kitchen. "What do you mean? I caught the evening news at six. Did that woman give another interview or something?"

"Ohhhhhh, yes." She handed me an iced martini glass with the divine pink mixture, then sipped from her crystal glass, filled, most likely, with her favorite bourbon. "I recorded it so you could see for yourself."

I could tell from her tone of voice that this interview would not be pleasant to watch. So I took a large sip of my Cosmo as I followed Samantha down the hall to her library office. On an empty stomach, the vodka would hit me fast. "I have a feeling I'm not gonna like this."

She picked up the television remote control. "Friends have been calling all day. They're mad as hell. Unfortunately, I've stepped on a lot of toes in this town over the years, so all those folks are rubbing their hands in glee, no doubt." She pushed more buttons and the TV video footage ran backwards for a few seconds, then started to play.

I sank into a moss green velvet upholstered armchair near Samantha's and watched as a news anchor appeared. "What channel is this? I don't recognize the people."

She leaned back in her chair. "That's because it's not local, it's a tabloid TV program. All the sleaze that's fit to broadcast. If it's on tape, it's good enough." She took another sip. "And here we go."

I watched as another reporter appeared beside the woman I recognized from the local evening news program I'd seen earlier. Widow Wilson, looking as composed and professional as before. "Great outfit, by the way. I can smell the money over the airwaves."

"Oh, yeah," Samantha smiled. "Quent was always making jokes about her clothing bills. Now, it starts."

The reporter held the microphone toward Widow Wilson and she proceeded to repeat the concerns she'd expressed earlier. She'd spoken with the police and wanted her husband's death "fully investigated" because she had "questions." The reporter probed, asking her if she doubted it was suicide. At that point, Widow Wilson looked straight at the camera and answered, clearly addressing more than the reporter.

"I do not believe my husband committed suicide. That's why I want police to thoroughly question the woman who owns the home where Quentin died. I have no doubt this woman was with him when he died. And this woman needs to tell police what she knows. Quentin confessed to me about their affair that very evening. And he was flying home to Ohio to see me the next day. Those are not the actions of a man who's about to commit suicide."

"Do you have any idea of the identity of this woman? Could you share that with us?" the reporter asked.

"I know who she is. And this woman owes it to those of us who're grieving Quentin's untimely death to confess what she knows. Tell the police the truth."

With that, Widow Wilson spun around and walked away between two men, who were hired security from the look of them. The tabloid reporter, clearly salivating for more, sputtered and called her name again and again, only to be ignored. Then he turned to the cameras again.

"Well, there will certainly be more to this story. Back to you, Miranda."

Still stunned by what I'd seen, I stared at the television as Samantha clicked off the screen. "Good God . . ." was all I could manage. Then I took a really large gulp of my Cosmo, feeling the vodka rush through my veins.

"That's what I said," she agreed then took another drink.

I looked over at my friend. "You know what you have to do, Samantha."

She closed her eyes and closed her hands around the crystal glass. "I won't do it, Molly. I won't compromise my dear friend."

The vodka egged me on. "Dammit, Sa-

117

mantha, be sensible. If this dear friend really cares about you, then he won't want to see you dragged through the mud. That's what's going to happen now, and you know it. Sneers and innuendoes won't be enough for the vultures. They're waiting in the trees ready to swoop down on you. You can't simply stand there and let them do it. Protect yourself! Give the police his name, *dammit!*"

Samantha looked over at me and smiled. "You're cute when you get mad. I know you're trying to protect me, sugar, but it's already too late. Word is spreading around town even as we speak. I can almost hear the buzz. Too late to stop it." She took a deep drink.

"That's the cicada outside," I countered, frustrated that she wouldn't listen to reason. "You know police are going to question you again. If for nothing else than to humor the grieving widow." I gestured toward the blank television screen.

Samantha stared into her glass. "They already have. That was why my lawyer called when we last talked. He and I went over to the police department in Fairfax this afternoon. It was quite an experience, I'll say that."

My stomach clenched despite the vodka.

"Oh no. What kinds of questions did they ask this time?"

"In addition to asking me where I was that night and who I was with, they wanted to know more about Quentin's prescription pill habit. Particularly what I knew about the young man my surveillance video captured on the day Quentin died. They said the medical examiner found opiate-based prescription drugs in Quentin's system along with sleeping pills. I told them everything I knew, which was exactly what I told you. It isn't much. I never knew his name, just that he was some research staffer who delivered Quentin's pills."

"Did they act like they believed you?"

She shrugged. "It's hard to tell. But I did notice their tone of voice was decidedly colder this time. Chilling, actually. I definitely felt they were looking at me with suspicion."

I leaned my head back on the chair. "Damn, damn, damn . . ."

"That's about what my lawyer said. Not in so many words." She gave me a wry smile.

I scowled at her. "This isn't a joke, Samantha. Your lawyer is as worried as I am. More so, I'm sure. *You're* the only one who's not worried. I'll bet your army of mice are chewing their little mousey toenails

119

off, worrying. Everyone who cares about you is panicked. Everyone but you." I drained my glass and pictured Samantha's bevy of confidantes and informants spread throughout the city. Unfortunately, this situation called for more than gathering info.

"Believe me, Molly, I'm not laughing. They also asked me how often I saw Quentin taking the Vicodin. I told them I didn't know for sure since I wasn't with him all the time. He kept the pills in his briefcase. But I had seen him use them occasionally when he was all wound up and couldn't get to sleep. With that terrible insomnia problem he had, anything that got Quentin all riled up would set him off. And between you and me, Quentin had been pretty wound up those last few weeks." She drained her glass. "Here, let me refill that." She reached for my empty glass as she rose from her chair.

"What was Quentin all wound up about? Was his wife starting to give him hell? Do you think she'd learned about you and Quentin a few weeks ago?"

Samantha walked over to one of the tall cherry wood bookcases and opened a discreetly concealed liquor cabinet. "No, Quentin would have told me if she had. He was all upset about something he'd overheard about a month ago. He was at some function in the State department and had stepped into a sitting room to nurse a headache. Quentin said he was seated in a tall armchair on the other side of the room, massaging his temple, when a Congressman and some European man suddenly came into the room. They must have been at this reception, too, because they started talking about a banking bill coming up in the Congressman's committee." She reached into the small fridge and withdrew another martini glass, already filled with my beverage of choice and handed it to me.

I took a sip of the yummy drink. "I can't believe you kept another Cosmo in there for me."

"Always prepared, you know me," Samantha smiled. "Anyway, Quentin said this foreign guy was really concerned about when the bill would be passed in committee. Well, that got Quentin's attention, and he figured he'd better stay quiet so they wouldn't discover he was there. God forbid the powerful chairman of an important congressional committee found a lowly Midwestern congressman eavesdropping on him." Samantha poured a couple of fingers worth of bourbon into her glass.

Meanwhile, her last sentence stopped the

martini glass at my lips. The words *powerful chairman of an important congressional committee* got my attention, even through the vodka. "Who was the congressman? Did Quentin say?"

Samantha walked back to her chair, sat down, then took a drink before answering. "I'm afraid he was your old nemesis. Edward Ryker."

That name and the memories it evoked burned through the vodka in my veins. Old nemesis, indeed. "What was that bill they were talking about again?"

"Some banking bill is all Quentin heard, but the fact that this European guy was so anxious about it captured Quent's curiosity. That, plus the way Congressman Ryker was talking to this guy. Quent said it sounded like Ryker was reassuring him, saying something like, 'it's going to be fine' and 'don't worry.' Oh, yes, and 'tell them I've got it under control.' " Samantha gave a little shrug. "That caught Quent's attention, and after that, he was like a dog with a bone. He wouldn't leave it alone." She took a deep drink of her bourbon.

I pondered the words Samantha remembered Wilson saying. *Don't worry. Tell them I've got it under control.* What was the "it" they referred to?

"They had to be talking about some bill in Ryker's committee," I said after a moment. "He's Chairman of the House Financial Services Committee. But why would Wilson get so interested? Banking bills were not his area, were they? He wasn't on any congressional financial committee, was he?"

"Nope. He was on the House Energy and Commerce Committee. In fact, I asked him the very same thing. Suddenly, Quent started researching banking legislation and all sorts of stuff outside his area. I told him he shouldn't be wasting his time." She shook her head. "But Quent was like that. He'd get all wrapped up in something and couldn't let it go. He was obsessive that way. I'd warned him to be careful, because he could step on powerful toes. But he wouldn't listen."

I sipped my Cosmo as old memories beckoned to me from the past. Old enemies and old battles. I'd had some obsessions of my own years ago after Dave's death. But I'd finally been able to break free of that anger and resentment and live in the present. I wasn't about to step into that quagmire again. Still, I couldn't help wondering what Quent Wilson overheard that fascinated him so much? Who was Congressman Ryker talking to? Could it have possibly been Ambassador Holmberg? He'd been a European Finance Minister.

Suddenly, memories of my recently murdered niece Karen Grayson rushed into my head. Still painful and raw. Karen's day-timer had written notations about Ambassador Holmberg speaking to various members of congress. And Danny and I had seen Ryker and Holmberg together with other political types at a Washington reception last spring. Karen had also been researching an organization, the Epsilon Group, that concentrated on global financial policy. Karen said that some of their policies had made it into the legislative process and had become laws. Maybe that's what the conversation Wilson overhead was all about. But what was so intriguing about a financial bill that would entice Wilson to spend his valuable time researching it?

No answers came. I took another deep drink of my Cosmo, feeling the vodka re-awaken in my veins and chase those old niggling thoughts from the edges of my mind.

I needed to stay in the present. Samantha had some very real problems staring her in the face. Serious problems. I smiled over at my old friend. "Okay, that's enough with the news, tawdry and otherwise. I say we raid your refrigerator for some of those gourmet leftovers, then find a good trashy movie and escape for a while. How about it?"

Samantha smiled and picked up the remote control once again. "Sounds good to me. If there're no trashy ones, why don't we watch one of those blow-em-up, shoot-em-up war movies? I learned to love those living with Beau."

I laughed out loud as I followed Samantha from the library.

Eight

Friday

The early morning sunshine filtered through the leaves overhead, casting shadows and light along the Chesapeake and Ohio Canal as I ran along the towpath. I depended on these early morning runs, the quiet time helped me sort through my thoughts, work out problems, and worry if necessary. Even when Danny joined me, we ran mostly in silence, saving our talking for postrun breakfasts at a French café along Georgetown's M Street.

Striding along the packed dirt path, I spied another runner farther ahead. I'd already passed two women a few minutes ago. Thanks to running with Danny, my pace had increased gradually. That sly fox had picked up his pace little by little until I was running faster. Of course, I'm sure Danny had to downshift just so that I could try and keep up with him. "Throttle back" as he called it.

Rush hour traffic clogged busy M Street above, as it paralleled the canal. It was far enough away so that I could still hear morning birdsong as I ran along. Not as peaceful as my Georgetown townhouse garden, but —

My office cell phone rang, shattering the morning quiet and birdsong. I quickly dug it from my running shorts' inner pocket and saw Peter Brewster's name and number flash on the screen. That was why I carried the phone wherever I went. No telling when Peter would call me.

"Good morning, Peter. The closer it gets to August recess, the earlier you get to the office."

"Oh, yeah. It's only seven ten and I'm already behind. Are you outside running?"

"Yep. Gotta grab these early summer mornings before the heat builds. What do you need? I left that file you gave me on your desk before I left last night. I'll be in the office in a little while if you need anything else."

"Actually what I need is some of your time tonight. I'd promised Eleanor MacKenzie that I'd stop by her charity fundraiser with the Senator's check and mine. Would you be able to go in my place? I know that's asking a lot. You probably have a date with Danny. I'll be leaving for the Hill in a minute. The Senator's already there. He and I will be buried in meetings with the Banking Committee staff all day and into the evening."

"Actually I'm free as a bird tonight. Danny's still out of town, and I was going to do errands, that's all. But I'd much rather go to Eleanor's fundraiser and deliver your contributions."

"Fantastic! Thanks, Molly. I'll put an envelope with the checks on your desk before I head for the Hill. The Senator and I are leaving for Colorado late tonight. So, we'll see you on Monday."

"Enjoy Colorado. Temps will be hot, but there'll be low humidity. You'll love it."

"Believe me, we always love escaping to Colorado," he said with a laugh before clicking off.

I checked my watch. Time to head home. I would have to hurry to shower, dress, and walk to Senator Russell's home by eight o'clock. Spying stone stair steps leading to the main streets above, I angled toward them, leaving the peaceful sunshine and water behind as I picked up my pace.

The string quartet finished with a vibrant

chord that shimmered in the air, floating above Eleanor MacKenzie's glorious garden. Flower beds, shrubs, vining trellises, all meticulously pruned and tended, manicured in the manner of yesteryear. An authentic English garden. I always loved an excuse to attend one of Eleanor's musical evenings, but her charity fundraisers were a little rich for my blood, and more importantly, my bank account. Thanks to Peter Brewster, however, I was able to revel in the lavish spread Eleanor was famous for and be the bearer of gifts at the same time.

Of course, politicians and politicos of all stripes were also mixed among the business elite and other movers and shakers of Washington. All of them bending elbows and gossiping or stabbing someone in the back — figuratively, of course. It hurt just the same. Tonight, I sensed my friend Samantha's recent notoriety was providing rich fodder for many. Consequently, I'd deliberately shied away from joining any clusters, choosing instead to speak with several new freshmen Congressional couples that I recognized. Still adjusting to the Washington social scene, their conversation would cover safer ground.

I passed by the table that held the constantly changing hors d'oeuvres and gave in to the temptation of a rich pate. As I sipped my Sauvignon Blanc, I noticed a friendly face smiling at me. Congresswoman Sally Chertoff headed my way. I angled away from the table so we could be far from the grazing herds.

"Congresswoman, how nice to see you," I greeted as she approached. "It's a wonder you were able to escape all that committee work you've undertaken."

"I feel like I'm playing hooky," she said, her square face lit up with her wide, bright smile. "But my staff insisted I take a break. And I'm so glad I took their advice. That quartet is fabulous, and I've had the most amazing canapés. I must have gained two pounds at least." She laughed lightly.

"You can always depend on Eleanor to have the best musicians and the best caterers. Her functions are always a joy. I'm here in place of Senator Russell and Peter, bearing charitable gifts for the worthy cause." I grinned. "They're both leaving for Colorado tonight."

"Well, I'll be leaving for Iowa in the wee hours tomorrow morning. I simply had to finish some projects that ran late into the afternoon." She sipped her red wine and glanced about the garden. "This is absolutely gorgeous. Eleanor MacKenzie has impeccable taste. When I grow up I want to be her." She laughed again.

"Hey, that's my line," I teased. "Changing the subject, I heard that you hired a new staffer last week. Natasha Jorgensen, Quentin Wilson's former chief. I've heard good things about her."

"Yes, indeed, I grabbed Natasha as soon as one of my staff hinted she was looking to jump ship. Natasha is whip smart, and I was impressed with her when Quentin and I worked together on a project." Her expression saddened. "He will be greatly missed. What a loss."

I pondered how to broach the subject and where I wanted to take it, deciding to nibble around the edges first. "I never really knew Congressman Wilson. I'd only seen him at the large reception Senator Russell gave for the Midwestern congressional delegation last spring. But it certainly was a shock to hear that he died so suddenly."

Sally Chertoff frowned. "I still cannot understand why Quentin would take his own life. He was so committed to his work and the people in his district of Ohio. It must have been accidental. That's the only way I can fathom how this happened."

"None of us can ever know the pressures others are under," I ventured. "We all become expert at hiding those concerns from everyone. Particularly those close to us."

Chertoff glanced at me. "You're right about that. The Virginia police detectives investigating Quentin's death actually came to the office yesterday and interviewed Natasha. Apparently, they had more questions about Quentin's prescription drug habits. Natasha was quite shaken by the entire episode. She told me afterwards that police asked if Quentin was using any other drugs, like prescription painkillers. Natasha had to tell them that he was. She'd seen the pill bottles on his desk."

I pretended to look surprised. "Oh, my, that does change things, doesn't it? If Wilson was mixing powerful painkillers with sleeping pills, that's a lethal mixture."

"Absolutely. That's why I suspect Quentin's death was accidental. If he was worrying about something, who knows?" Chertoff stared into her wineglass, not venturing any more.

I sensed the congresswoman had deliberately not said more, so I used that as an opportunity to venture into more controversial territory. "Well, considering what we all witnessed on the news channels Wednesday, I'd say Quentin Wilson had a lot to worry about. His widow certainly comes across as a powerful woman. If she'd gotten word of an affair, well . . . I imagine Wilson would hear from her. Loud and clear."

Sally Chertoff glanced up with a wry smile. "Yes, she seems quite imposing."

"There are rumors she plans to take over Wilson's seat for the remainder of his term. Assuming Ohio's governor agrees, that is," I said in a deliberately sardonic tone.

Chertoff's eyes lit up. "Yes, Natasha confirmed that's true. That's why she jumped ship. Apparently, Mrs. Wilson let it be known when she visited the office that she would ask the Governor to appoint her to Quentin's seat. And she would bring some Ohio staff with her. I've also heard she's been meeting with other members of Congress from both sides of the aisle. Apparently she has a list of people to meet. Her father's been involved with Ohio politics for nearly thirty years. So, she has a great many connections." Chertoff gave a wry smile.

"Imposing *and* organized. A good combination." I decided a lighter note offered me the chance to steer the conversation where I wanted it. Those nagging little questions from my visit to Samantha's Wednesday evening hadn't gone away. "I've had a chance to observe the Widow Wilson from another perspective, so I'm more than a little intrigued by her plans. Samantha Calhoun is one of my oldest and dearest friends. She and I grew up together in Washington's crucible as Senators' daughters years ago. We're very close, so I'm sure you can understand I was rather concerned when I heard Mrs. Wilson's pointed comments about Congressman Wilson and his 'evening companion,' as she put it." I held Sally Chertoff's direct gaze. "Samantha and Wilson had a very close relationship, and apparently Mrs. Wilson learned about it the day Wilson overdosed on pills."

Sally Chertoff watched me intently. "I confess, I had heard rumors as to the identity of Quentin's companion that night. So it *was* Samantha Calhoun's house where he died?"

"Yes, and it was Samantha who found him early the next morning. You can imagine her shock and horror."

Chertoff's surprised blue eyes stared back. "So she *wasn't* there when Wilson took the pills? Then Mrs. Wilson is deliberately slandering Mrs. Calhoun. She will have to respond."

I gave her a rueful smile. "Unfortunately, Samantha has chosen not to respond. That's not her style, which makes her a perfect target for someone who's anxious to establish a presence in Washington. Gossip and innuendo are practically spectator sports here. Perception is reality in Washington."

"I'm sorry to hear that," the congresswoman said, her expression conveying her sincerity. "I've never met Mrs. Calhoun, but I know several of her friends speak highly of her. She's been quite generous in contributing to their charities. I also hate to see bullies succeed. We really don't need more of them in the arena."

I decided to gamble on Chertoff's sympathetic comment. "Samantha had high praise for Natasha. She called her 'Quentin's right arm.' Even saying you were lucky to have her." I paused. "In fact, she told me she called Natasha after Wilson's death and asked if she had noticed any signs of depression or comments that last day he was alive. Apparently Wilson was working at his office before going to Samantha's to retrieve his things."

"Yes, Natasha told me she blamed herself for not picking up any signals that Quentin might end his life. I told her I doubted there were any signals to see. Quentin Wilson accidentally took too many pills. And judging from what we've seen on the news channels, we can all understand the stress he must have been under." Chertoff smiled just a bit. "That was kind of Mrs. Calhoun to reassure Natasha."

"As I said, Samantha thinks highly of her." I chose my next words carefully, sensing this would be a good time to pose my request. "Do you think it's possible for me to meet Natasha? I promise I won't disturb your office routine. I simply had a couple of questions involving some research that Wilson was doing before he died. It involved financial legislation currently before the House. My niece Karen Grayson was researching some similar legislation before . . . before she died." I deliberately looked away. "She spoke to me about it the very day she was killed. I decided to follow up on her research. I suppose it's sort of my own little tribute to her."

"Of course, Molly. I wouldn't mind at all, and I'm sure Natasha would be happy to help you, especially because of Karen. Sonia, my chief of staff, was also a friend of Karen's. She and Karen went on some weekend shopping excursions with Natasha and other staffers." Her expression turned sorrowful again. "It was dreadful what happened to Karen. I can't tell you how heartsick many of us were at her death. I'd had a chance to work with Randall Jackson's office on legislation that benefitted both our states several times. We were neighbors. It was tragic, simply tragic."

"Thank you, Congresswoman, for your kind words. Karen was a shining light, and I still miss her." Feeling those old thoughts of loss creep around the edges of my mind, I deliberately returned to the present. The Ugly Past scuttled back to the bushes. "Should I call your office and make an appointment with Natasha?"

"You won't have to, Molly. Natasha and Sonia are here at the fundraiser," she said with a smile. "I figured it was the best way to help Natasha shake off the unpleasant police questions. And Sonia jumps at any of Eleanor MacKenzie's invitations." She looked over her shoulder toward the people crowding Eleanor's gardens and shady walkways. "I told them to go off and wander on their own. No need to follow me around . . . there they are — beside that fountain. Come along, I'll introduce you. You and Natasha can have a few minutes to yourselves in one of Eleanor's precious corners or garden enclosures."

"Perfect. Now I won't have to disturb your office routine," I said, following in Sally Chertoff's wake as she wove a path around

Eleanor's guests. I drained the last of my wine and deposited the empty glass on a passing server's tray.

Spying two young women standing together a few feet from a table laden with new canapés and delicious tempting appetizers, I figured they were Chertoff's staffers, clearly enjoying themselves.

"Molly, I'd like you to meet my chief of staff, Sonia Werner, and Natasha Jorgensen, who's newly come over from Quentin Wilson's office," Chertoff said as we walked up to them. "Sonia, Natasha, meet Molly Malone. She's on Senator Russell's staff."

Sonia offered her hand first, and we all exchanged greetings.

"Molly wanted to meet you, Natasha. She was Karen Grayson's aunt, if you recall. You may remember her if you attended Karen's funeral service last spring."

The blond turned toward me immediately, her pretty face devoid of the happier expression. "Yes, I do recognize you from the service. Karen was a good friend and a mentor to me when I first came to the Hill. I was devastated by her death. It was simply tragic." Her young face clouded over.

"As were we all, Ms. Jorgensen. Thank you for those memories of Karen. That sounds like her."

"Ms. Malone has a few questions she wanted to ask you about Quentin Wilson's last research projects, Natasha. It appears Karen was researching some similar subjects. Molly wants to finish Karen's project, sort of in tribute to her. Do I have that right, Molly?" She glanced my way with a smile.

"I couldn't have said it better, Congresswoman. I promise I won't take more than a few minutes of your time, Natasha. I don't want to take you away from Eleanor's delightful surroundings very long." I gave her a bright smile.

"I enjoyed talking with you, Molly, as usual." Chertoff grinned. "And give my best to your old friend. I'm rooting for her." She walked away, her chief staffer by her side.

"Which research project was Karen working on, Ms. Malone?" Natasha asked as we both edged away from an approaching group heading toward the canapés. Eleanor must be spending a fortune tonight.

"She was curious about some financial legislation that might be coming up before the House," I said, heading toward one of the curving brick pathways that skirted the grounds of Eleanor's Cleveland Park estate. "I recall her mentioning it when we had breakfast together the last day she was alive. I know that may sound strange, trying to follow up on some vague comment." I deliberately gave a little shrug. "Maybe it's my way of keeping Karen's memory alive. She was such a perfectionist and a stickler for finishing any project she started."

"Yes, she was. Karen was a tremendous role model for me, Ms. Malone —"

"Please, call me Molly. We're all in this crazy business of politics and politicians. So, we all work for the same company, so to speak."

She grinned. "Okay, Molly. As to those research projects, most of Congressman Wilson's legislative research concentrated on his Energy and Commerce committee work. But I do recall the congressman expressing interest in some financial legislation several weeks ago. I remember thinking it a little strange because he'd never been interested in that area before. He was very focused and targeted on what impacted his Ohio constituents."

"Do you remember any details in particular?" I probed. "Was there a specific bill he was interested in?"

Natasha shook her head. "No, I don't. I'm sorry, Molly. But I can point you to someone who may have more specific details. She's a senior researcher in the Congressional Research Service. Congressman Wilson always tried to get on her schedule. I can't remember her name, but I can find it for you when I'm back at Congresswoman Chertoff's office. I have my day scheduler and records from Wilson's office in a drawer, because I can tell I'm going to be answering a myriad of questions when Sylvia Wilson is appointed to finish the term."

I couldn't miss the brief flash of irritation that appeared on the young woman's face. "I'm sure you will be, Natasha," I gave her a wicked smile. "Judging from that performance on the evening news Wednesday night, the Widow Wilson seems quite the diva."

Natasha's smile escaped. "You have no idea."

"It was also smart to keep all your records," I added. "Protection, so to speak." I decided to venture a little more. "You know, Samantha Calhoun is a very dear friend of mine. We grew up together here in the hothouse of Washington politics. Both our fathers were Senators. So, you can imagine my reaction to the Widow Wilson's performance on the evening news. Let's hope her fifteen minutes of fame are over."

Natasha's eyes danced. "Don't bet on it. That woman has plans, trust me. And I certainly wasn't going to be included.

Clearly, she's bringing her Ohio lackeys with her. Let's see how long they last on the Hill."

I laughed. "You know, Samantha had very complimentary things to say about you. For the record, she's glad you're in Chertoff's office. She said Congresswoman Chertoff was lucky to have you. You were Quentin Wilson's right arm."

Natasha glanced into her empty wineglass. "Samantha Calhoun is a lovely person. I've met her at some political fundraisers. Please tell her I appreciate her kind thoughts."

I debated my next words. "Samantha told me she called you after Wilson's death. She said you were just as shocked by Wilson's pill overdose as she was."

"Yes, we spoke. It was nice of her to call. She wound up reassuring me and said not to blame myself for missing a signal that wasn't there."

"That sounds like Samantha. You know, I'm curious about something, Natasha. I'd heard that Wilson was using prescription painkillers too. That's a lethal combination with sleeping pills. How long had Wilson been using them?"

Natasha looked up, and her gaze turned anxious. "I'm not sure exactly. I just saw the pills on his desk." Her glance darted away.

"That was a tragic mistake on his part," I said, intrigued by her reaction.

"Yes . . . yes, it was," she said softly, glancing into her wineglass again, clearly nervous.

I sensed there was something else she could have said, but chose not to. I didn't push it. "I'm sorry I asked, Natasha. I can see all of this brings back unpleasant memories." I began to back away. "Go rejoin your friend and enjoy Eleanor's hospitality. You've been very kind to answer my questions. Thank you so much."

"You're more than welcome, Molly." Natasha's smile returned. "I've enjoyed talking with you. Let's hope Senator Russell has another reception for Midwesterners. Maybe I'll see you then."

"You definitely will. Shepherding politicos at the Senator's various functions is one of the best parts of my job. Of course, getting to live in Georgetown is another perk, I admit. I live only a few blocks from the Senator's Q Street home, so I get to walk to and from the office." I purposely started strolling in the general direction that Congresswoman Chertoff and her staffer Sonia had walked.

Natasha fell into step beside me. "Boy, are

you lucky! I'd almost open a vein to live there. I was hoping to find a house to share with several roommates so we could afford it. I love that area. Plus all the great cafes and shopping all around."

"I know what you mean. It's all too easy to go shopping after work. Of course, whenever I feel that urge and my bank account isn't cooperating, I go running along the Canal instead. Works every time. Of course, I don't take my credit card running."

"Don't you love running by the Canal," she said, waving at her fellow staffer Sonia across the rosebushes. "I run there every morning between Rock Creek and Key Bridge."

"Really? So do I. Funny I haven't seen you. I'm usually there around six or six thirty."

"I confess I'm an early bird," she said, backing away. "I try to start my run around five thirty or so. I'm at the Hill by seven."

"I'm impressed. Take care, Natasha, maybe I'll see you there some morning," I said as she walked away.

The string quartet struck a couple of short chords, indicating they were about to commence play once more. I noticed several of Eleanor's guests edge away from the food and meander across the grass toward the upper patio where the musicians were seated. Eleanor's mansion had an Old World style that suited her. The upper patio jutted out from the upstairs sitting room. The downstairs patio off the main room was filled with the catering staff who were carrying what looked like serving trays of desserts.

I debated leaving to avoid the temptation of what would undoubtedly be a wickedly sinful assortment of calories. I'd had a few moments when I arrived earlier in the evening to chat with Eleanor. I could tell from her expression she wanted to speak more but couldn't under the circumstances. As hostess of this grand fundraiser, she had no time for anything more than brief conversations with her many guests.

Certainly there was no time for a discussion about our mutual dear friend Samantha Calhoun's current predicament. That would take a great deal more time, indeed.

NINE

Tuesday

Larry Fillmore took the Metro escalator steps two at a time as he climbed upward, phone pressed to his ear. "I just had a call from Gary Levitz," he said, moving away from the early morning crowds emerging from the Capitol South Metro station. "A friend at the *Dirt* called him last night and gave a head's up about today's issue. He's panicked and wants to get out of town fast. I told him to grab all the cash he could get his hands on, and I'd call him back in a couple hours. Meanwhile, he should take a cab to Reagan National Airport and wait for my call. Promised him I'd have an out-of-town contact lined up."

"Good, good," Spencer replied. "I'll call Raymond and get him on it right away. He'll handle arrangements. I'll let you know where to meet him so he can fill you in. So, make sure you don't get tied down in meetings this morning."

Larry strode across New Jersey Avenue, the Rayburn Office Building two blocks ahead. "That will be tricky. Jackson's in committee meetings this morning. I'm supposed to go with him," he protested, annoyed. "I'm his chief of staff, remember?"

"Send someone else. Call in sick, a dental emergency, whatever. Just be available, got it?"

Spencer didn't ask, he directed; Larry noticed. "Got it," he echoed.

"I'll call as soon as I hear from Raymond."

Trying once more to salvage his morning, Larry ventured. "Why don't you just have Raymond call *me*. He can give me the details over the phone. It'll be faster."

Spencer's deep voice chuckled. "Raymond only calls me."

Larry kept his mouth shut as he turned around and headed back toward the metro station. Meanwhile, he clicked on his office phone number. Dental emergency, it was.

"Molly, there's some coffee left if you're interested," Casey said, leaning inside my office. "Luisa made a fresh pot."

Music to my ears. I grabbed my empty mug and pushed away from my desk. Only eight thirty-five and I needed to escape the computer screen already. It was going to be a long day. "I'll need another mug to finish all these e-mails."

"Don't you just love mornings," Casey joked as we walked down the stretch of polished walnut hallway.

"Ohhhh, yeah. It's been fun ever since I turned on my kitchen TV and caught the morning news. Boy, the Widow Wilson must have hit every news outlet in the D.C. metro Area. I expect to see her on the Shopping Channel next."

Casey snickered over his mug. "Widow Wilson. I gotta admit, she's something else. She was everywhere these last few days."

"Tell me about it." I rounded the corner into Luisa's immaculate kitchen. The wide windows on the east side let the morning sun pour in. Morning sun always cheered me up.

"How's your friend holding up under the widow's media blitz?"

I pulled the urn's lever and watched the hot black stream pour into my mug, aroma wafting to my nostrils. The caffeine lobe of my brain responded on scent alone. "Pretty well, considering. She's basically staying home and keeping out of the public eye for a while. That's hard for her, because Samantha is someone who's always going somewhere. She's got groups and meetings all over town." I took a sip, hot and strong.

"That's probably a good idea for now. Mrs. Wilson is bound to go back to Ohio sometime."

"She'll go back, but she won't stay," I jibed, taking another sip. "I hear she's going to be appointed to finish out her husband's term. So, the Widow Wilson will be amongst us. What a happy thought." I made a face.

Casey looked genuinely surprised. "No kidding! Brother, she must have a lot of connections."

"Old Ohio money, and she's tight with the Governor. I'd say that's a sure bet."

"By the way, my old Marine buddy with the Fairfax cops gave me a call yesterday. He said that your friend Samantha has definitely gotten the attention of the detective who's investigating Quentin Wilson's death. And not in a good way. She's still not revealing the name of the person she was with the night Wilson overdosed. I don't have to tell you that didn't set well with those guys."

I released a long aggravated sigh. "I can imagine. I remember how the Arlington cops used to scare me when I was a kid years ago. They'd ride past on their motor-cycles, staring through their shades. All they had to do was look your way, and you felt guilty. I swear to God." I shook my head as long-ago images of those tough-looking cops darted through my head.

Casey chuckled. "Yeah, I remember some of those guys. Most of them were Korean vets and tough as nails. You didn't mess with them. My friends and I made sure we stayed way across the bridge in D.C." His dark face lost its smile and that worried expression reappeared. "You gotta convince Samantha to tell the cops the truth, Molly. The stakes have been raised now. The medical examiner found opiates in Wilson's bloodstream along with the sleeping pills, and they found a bottle of Vicodin on the floor and an empty mailing envelope with Wilson's name on it."

I leaned against the counter. "Samantha told me the police revealed the medical examiner's report when she and her lawyer went in for more questioning the other day. And they asked her a whole lot of questions about Wilson's pill habit. Samantha told them everything she knew."

"Well, that's good, but she still has to come clean about her whereabouts that night."

"Believe me, Casey, I nagged her a lot the other evening. I actually stayed over because I didn't want her alone that night after that awful woman had spouted off on all the news channels." I scowled into my mug. "Dammit. Samantha is paying a high price for her brand of loyalty."

Casey's worried expression deepened. "Well, let's hope she comes to her senses because she's still at the top of the Fairfax cops' list. All because she won't explain where she was. My friend says investigators are wondering if she stayed with Wilson that night. Of course, that opens up all kinds of speculation."

I closed my eyes. "Oh, no . . ."

"Police can't rule out anything, Molly. Apparently, they're taking another look at all of the information they have. Including everything they found in Wilson's briefcase and his office."

I considered what Casey said. Did that mean the surveillance photos of Samantha and Wilson? Wilson must have had them in his briefcase, so the cops found them right away. Samantha said the police told her lawyer the photos were being held in a safe place. "Did your friend mention any photographs?" I asked.

Casey's left brow shot up. "No, he didn't. What kind of photographs?"

"The very worst kind, Casey. Private investigator, peek-behind-bedroom-curtains kind of photographs. Samantha and Wilson, caught in the act at her Winchester estate. Samantha told me that Wilson received a courier-delivered package the morning of his death. He called her after discovering the photos. A little while later, Samantha received the same package. They decided to break off their affair immediately. That's why Wilson was at Samantha's that evening. He went to retrieve his personal belongings."

"Any idea who sent those photos? Any information on the mailer label?"

I shook my head. "No, Samantha said Wilson checked on the company listed, something funny sounding, like Acme, Inc. It was bogus. No company listed with that name. And that Indiana address didn't turn up anything either. So it was deliberately misleading."

"Someone's either very smart or very careful. Probably both." He thought for a second. "Does she think it could be the Widow Wilson?"

"Yeah, both Samantha and I think his wife sent the photos. Mainly because neither Samantha nor Wilson received a blackmail message. Nothing, just the photos. If money was the reason someone took the photos, there would be a demand in a note or an e-mail. Neither one received a note. So, the only other reason would be to intimidate Wilson. Plus, the Widow Wilson has the money to hire professional investigators. Samantha said those photos had to have been taken from a distance because she has security fencing all around her property." I paused. "Do you think the police found a message or something at Wilson's office or in his briefcase?"

Casey smiled. "I asked my friend the same thing. He said he wasn't at liberty to say."

"Hmmmmm. That makes me curious. It sounds as if they did find something and maybe it implicates Widow Wilson."

"Or, maybe it's vague enough to implicate your friend Samantha, too," Casey said, giving me a stern look. "All the more reason Samantha needs to remove herself from this investigation entirely by telling police where she was that night and with whom. Her lawyer must be tearing his hair out in frustration." He drained his coffee and refilled his cup.

"He's bald already, if I remember correctly. He's probably working on an ulcer right now. And so are all her friends."

Casey reached inside his jacket and pulled out the notorious local rag, placing it on the kitchen counter. "There's a new story here

I think you'll find interesting."

"All the sleaze that's fit to print, right?" I drained my mug and followed Casey's example, refilling it to the brim.

"In the 'Whispers & Rumors' column today, there was some anonymous tip about a Capitol Hill staffer who supplied prescription drugs to clients on the Hill. And it even mentioned Wilson as one of the so-called 'clients.' "

"Oh, brother. Now, they're going to trash Quentin Wilson's reputation. Next, they'll sharpen their knives and slice into Samantha."

"They've already started. I thought you'd seen it. Otherwise, I'd have said something."

"*Damn*. And this day was stressful to begin with." I took a deep drink of steaming coffee and felt it burn all the way down my throat. I picked up the newsprint and scowled. "I don't believe I'm gonna have to read this every day."

Casey chuckled as we left the kitchen. "Join the rest of us, Molly, and keep up with the gossip."

"You haven't been in this rag, Casey. *I have*," I countered, waving the tabloid as we turned down the hallway. "I'm going to read this garbage, then call Samantha."

"Give her hell, Molly. No more protecting

Mister No-Name. It's getting dangerous out there," Casey warned as he walked in the opposite direction.

I started in on my friend the moment she answered the phone. "I don't want to hear any more excuses, Samantha. You need to call your lawyer today and tell those Fairfax cops exactly where you were the night Wilson died."

"Well, hello, Molly," Samantha's contralto voice answered. I could hear the amusement in it.

"Don't argue with me. You have to protect yourself. The sharks are in the water now. Did you read that local rag, *D.C. Dirt*? They've already named you and called Wilson the latest in your list of numerous liaisons! Good God, Samantha! They even hinted you were there with him the night he died!"

"I know. I've been hearing from my friends all morning. They're convinced Sylvia Wilson is behind all those rumors. Apparently she was making the rounds of every party and gathering she could these last few days. I doubt the woman slept from the sound of it."

I heard the tiredness in Samantha's voice, so I pressed again. "It sounds like that woman has a personal vendetta against you. It's gotten more than nasty out there. Sylvia Wilson is vicious, and the only way you can stop her is to tell police where you were that night and with whom. Once you do, you'll shut her up for good. And the Widow Wilson will look like the vindictive bitch she is."

Samantha's soft laughter came over the phone. "You're such a fighter, Molly. You always stick up for your own."

"Always. And I've got the battle scars to prove it," I joked.

She laughed louder. "Bloodied, but unbowed, the two of us. Bless your heart. You can rest easy. When my lawyer called to give me hell this morning, I told him to schedule a meeting with the Fairfax County Police this afternoon. I'll tell them exactly where I was that night and with whom."

I released a long loud sigh. "Thank God, Samantha. I know you were giving Jefferson Carter ulcers. What'd he say to convince you? All of your friends have been pleading with you for days."

"Well, he reminded me if I thought my life was unpleasant now, that was nothing compared to what would happen if I became the chief suspect in a murder investigation. But it wasn't Jefferson who convinced me, actually. It was Julia."

I pictured Samantha's daughter, Julia Monroe, a talented pianist, supporter of the arts, and as unassuming and low-profile as Samantha was flamboyant. "Excellent. I'm curious. What'd she say?"

"Julia came to my house early this morning, right after she'd dropped both girls at school. I was still in my dressing gown, so I was surprised to say the least."

"And?"

"She announced we were going to have a 'Come to Jesus' meeting. Her words, not mine. She told me she'd been able to laugh off all the various whispers and rumors about my affairs over the years, but this incident was *not* laughable. Some of the things she'd read and heard this weekend brought tears to her eyes. And then . . . *then* she said someone at school had already whispered something ugly to Peyton. Well, I tell you, Molly, that did it. If anyone had tried to hurt my precious girls, I'd tear their throat out with my bare hands. And to think that I did it myself . . . well, I couldn't bear it. I dissolved in tears."

My heart ached for my dear friend. All of us had trespassed in one way or another over the years. Regrets and recriminations had become part of everyone's baggage. If we were fortunate, we learned how to lighten that load over time. But repentance wasn't for everyone. And redemption, only for the lucky few. Forgiveness . . . well, that was even harder. Often sought, seldom found. Especially for ourselves.

"Samantha, please don't beat up on yourself any more than you already have," I said in a soft voice. "We all make choices in life. Some choices are good, some aren't so good. But most of us don't have our actions spread out in the tabloid sleaze for all to see. We get to make our mistakes in private. You were simply unlucky. Much worse is going on in Washington right now, but it will stay behind closed doors. It'll never be out in the open for everyone to see."

"And here, I'd always considered myself lucky." I heard the smile return to Samantha's wet voice.

"And you are. You're healthy and have people that love you. Thank God for friends and family."

"Amen to that."

Her response brought an amusing image to my mind, and I knew it would make Samantha laugh. "Hey, if you really want to make this a 'new beginning' you could go to church. I'll even go with you. When's the last time you went? I can't even remember the last time I went to Mass."

"You've got to be joking. The two of us going to Mass?" Samantha burst into laughter. "Lord, girl, the earth would shake if we walked in there."

"Stained glass rattling in the windows, holy water splashing in the font," I continued, laughing at the images I'd created. "Hey, it would be fun!"

Samantha hooted with laughter again. "You are crazier than a bedbug, girl. I swear you are."

Hearing Samantha reply with one of her old phrases made me feel better. Samantha was wounded, but she'd recover. Bloodied but unbowed. The two of us.

"Listen, Eleanor MacKenzie is coming over this week for one of Russell's dinners. Is it all right if I tell her you're cooperating with police?"

"Sure, go ahead and tell the Queen Mother," she teased. "She's probably fit to be tied by now."

"I'm sure she is. She shot me a couple of looks the other night at that charity fundraiser she held. I could tell Eleanor was dying to talk to me but couldn't because of all the guests. So, I'd like to ease her mind. She really cares about you, Samantha."

"I know she does. The old dear. Go ahead,

Molly. By the way, you've never asked me who I was with that evening."

I heard the tease in her voice, so I played along. "Oh, I figured you'd tell me sooner or later. Tell me now, so I can update Eleanor. That way, we know the word will spread to all the *right* circles."

Samantha chuckled. "Good idea. My companion for that evening . . . and that night . . . was my dear old friend, Bernard Bergstrom."

I paused, for only a heartbeat. "*What!* Isn't he —"

"In the Administration? Yes, he's one of the President's foreign policy advisors."

"Ye Gods, Samantha!" I blurted. *"The Administration!* You've . . . you've always stayed within Congress! *What were you thinking?"*

"I have friends all over Washington. And in all three branches of Government." I heard the tease again.

"Dear God . . ." I muttered while Samantha laughed lightly. I could tell she was enjoying my reaction.

"Bernie is a wise man and I needed some of his sage counsel after I'd received those photos. He's seen his share of scandal over the years. He knows how to survive."

I glanced at my computer screen and saw all the messages blinking at me. "I've gotta get back to work. Listen, Miss Thing, I know we've got a tripartite government, but promise me you'll leave the Judiciary alone, okay?"

Samantha laughed so loud I had to hold the phone away from my ear.

TEN

Thursday evening

Danny's name flashed on my cell phone as I logged off my office computer. "Hey, there, I'm almost finished," I said as I shoved some files into a desk drawer. "Senator Russell and Peter arrived a few minutes ago, thank God. Otherwise, I'd be playing hostess for the dinner guests and making you wait. When's our reservation, again?"

"Don't worry about it, I'll tell them we'll be a little late," Danny's deep voice sounded. "Why don't I pick you up at Russell's? It'll save you time."

"Uhhhh, okay. I was going to change, but —"

"No need. You always look great." I heard the light in his voice, and it went right through me like always. Hard not to like a man who said things like that.

"Flattery, flattery," I teased, checking my makeup in the framed mirror beside the

162

bookcase. Grabbing my purse, I rifled through it with one hand, searching for my small makeup case. "I appreciate it after the day I've had."

"What have the politicos been up to while I've been gone? Their usual chaos?"

"Actually the politicos weren't the stars in this melodrama. Other players were making news. And Samantha had a leading role. I'll fill you in at dinner," I said as I touched up my makeup and fluffed my hair.

Danny laughed deep in his throat. That sound always made my pulse race. "I can't wait. I'm on Connecticut Avenue now. I should be there shortly."

"Give me ten minutes, okay?" I said, closing my office door and heading down the mansion's main hallway. "I've got to deliver a message to one of the dinner guests."

"Roger that." His phone clicked off.

The sound of voices beckoned to me from the living room. Since these dinners for Senate colleagues were deliberately smaller than Russell's earlier dinner events, there was a more intimate atmosphere, which was precisely what Senator John Russell told me he wanted. Only eight people around the table, talking and getting to know one another in a more relaxed setting.

I paused at the edge of the living room

and scanned the guests. Senator Russell was beside the fireplace, talking with my old friend, Senator Alan Baker, senior Republican on the Senate Banking Committee. Peter, who had just returned from a Hill staffer meeting a half hour ago, still managed to look relaxed while talking with Senator Baker's wife, Brenda. I spied the senator from Oregon and his lovely wife on the sofa, chatting with the senator from Missouri. And there, beside the bookcase, was Eleanor MacKenzie in her signature peach silk — couture, of course. She was speaking to a couple I couldn't recognize from the back.

I debated interrupting for a brief moment with Eleanor when she suddenly glanced my way. I smiled and pointed toward the hallway. Eleanor guessed my signal, and I watched as she excused herself from the couple and walked toward me in her queenly stride.

"Forgive me for interrupting, Eleanor, but I have good news to share, and you'll want to hear it."

Eleanor's bright blue gaze sharpened and focused on me. "Please tell me Samantha has explained her whereabouts during that dreadful evening when Congressman Wilson died."

I gave her a big grin. "Yes, she has, thank

goodness. Samantha and her lawyer, Jefferson Parker, spoke with the Fairfax County Police just the other day."

Eleanor closed her eyes in uncharacteristic fashion, which told me how worried she'd been. "Thank Heavens," she breathed. "I cannot tell you how upset I've been ever since it became known Congressman Wilson died at her home. That's when the rumors started, getting worse every day." She shuddered. "Horrible, simply horrible. And then that Ohio woman's ugly accusations. After that, the gossip turned even more malicious. Every place I went."

"I know. Samantha's stepped on a lot of toes in this town, and —"

Eleanor gave an unladylike snort. "*Humph!* She's done more than that. Samantha has engaged in outrageous liaisons with those younger congressmen, almost as if she was deliberately flouting . . ." Eleanor gestured, at an unusual loss for words.

"Propriety," I ventured, with a devilish smile.

Eleanor gave me a schoolmarm's look. "Yes, *propriety*. It may sound old-fashioned, but it still has value. I'm afraid Samantha's done irreparable damage to her reputation. There were many who envied the social standing she'd acquired in this city through her political connections and her considerable wealth. Some of them have been waiting gleefully for her to slip off that tightrope she was walking. Now that she has, and in such a public fashion, she will have a hard time re-establishing herself. That is, if Samantha chooses to." Eleanor arched an aristocratic brow in skepticism.

As always, my sophisticated mentor and confidante had hit the target question squarely. Surely Samantha wouldn't return to her wanton ways . . . would she? Her latest liaison with the elderly diplomat and advisor to presidents indicated that Samantha's ability to choose high-profile and controversial companions indicated she still enjoyed shocking the Powers That Be.

An idea wiggled out of the mist and danced through my mind suddenly. It was outrageous, but perhaps it would take something outrageous to counteract the damage Samantha had done to herself. "I couldn't agree with you more, Eleanor. Samantha has a lot of repair work to do, especially after being dragged through the mud in the news media. I have an idea that might help, but it would involve your cooperation."

"And what might that be, pray tell?" Both brows shot up this time as Eleanor eyed me.

"Perhaps you could take Samantha under your protective wing, so to speak," I suggested. "Have her accompany you to all the charitable functions and social events you attend every week. That ought to keep her busy and occupy her evenings at the same time. No free evenings for stray dalliances." I gave a wicked smile. "With your busy schedule, I predict Samantha will be exhausted. Which is not a bad thing, in this case."

Eleanor's smile started slowly until her eyes danced. "Molly, my dear, you're a woman after my own heart. What a brilliant idea. Positively diabolical. Have Samantha serve a very public penance for all to see."

"And how better than by your side, doing good deeds. Samantha already supports multiple charities. This would be a logical extension. More dramatic, of course, but this situation calls for a dramatic solution, don't you think?"

She nodded. "I agree with you, Molly. But the question is whether Samantha will agree to an arrangement like that. I rather suspect she will not. Samantha values her independence."

"Well, I'll wait for a good time to suggest it to her." I grinned. "Oh, by the way, she told me who her evening companion was and gave me permission to share it with you. That way, Eleanor's Network will have privileged information to share."

Eleanor's blue eyes danced again. "How considerate of you, Molly. Tell me, who was the lucky gentleman?"

"Bernard Bergstrom." I didn't have to wait long for her reaction.

Her eyes popped wide in a very un-Eleanorlike expression. *"Bernie Bergstrom!"* she whispered. "He was one of Beauregard's old pals. And he's advising the *President*!"

"Yes, I was as shocked as you. Samantha has usually kept her dalliances within the Legislative Branch."

Eleanor gave a low laugh. "A member of the Administration. And a Republican, to boot. My, my, Samantha's tastes have broadened over the years."

I couldn't resist teasing. "I have to admit that Senator Russell's Independent political status has rubbed off on me, so I think a little cross-party activity is beneficial."

Eleanor laughed out loud this time. "Will you be joining us for dinner? I sincerely hope so."

"No, I have dinner plans already," I said. I glanced at my watch and was surprised by the time. "In fact, he should —"

"I believe he's here now," Eleanor said,

gesturing behind me.

I turned around and saw Danny standing at the front door, talking to Albert. I started backing away from Eleanor. "Enjoy your evening, Eleanor. And Samantha gave permission to spread the word far and wide."

"I will do my best, my dear. Now get away from us and join that handsome man waiting for you. We'll talk again soon."

I took my mentor's advice and hastened to meet Danny.

I took another deep drink of the delectable pink nectar in the Martini glass. It was my second Cosmo. Spaced by a wonderful goat cheese salad and a delicious broiled snapper, which I picked at while updating Danny on the latest chapter of the Samantha Saga. Usually I stayed with wine when I was with Danny, but tonight I was so relieved about Samantha that I'd ordered my favorite poison without even thinking.

I glanced across the table at my dinner companion. Danny was sipping his scotch and smiling at me. That amused smile of his that lit up his dark eyes. I'd gotten really fond of that smile these last four months.

Suddenly, the realization that I'd spent the last half hour talking about Samantha registered despite the Cosmo cloud that cushioned me right now. "Sorry to go on about Samantha like that," I said.

"Don't apologize. You were worried about your friend. And with good reason. I'm glad Samantha finally came to her senses." He sipped his scotch. "Bernie Bergstrom, huh? I remember meeting him when he was an assistant to the Secretary of Defense. That was years ago, so Bergstrom must be in his eighties by now."

"Samantha has always had a fondness for older men. Powerful older men." I said with a sly smile, then drained my glass, letting that delightful vodka float take me. "This is the first time Samantha's left both the Legislative Branch and the Democrats for her extracurricular activities."

Danny laughed softly and placed his warm hand over mine. "You've got interesting friends, Molly. I'll say that."

The warmth of his hand penetrated even the vodka. So much so, I spoke without thinking. "I'm curious . . . why haven't you made a move on me?"

Danny's eyes lit up as he leaned over the table toward me. "I'm waiting."

I leaned forward, getting closer. "I guess Samantha was right. She said you were waiting for my signal." Encouraged that I'd finally ventured into the territory I'd been dancing around for months, I waved my hand. "Consider yourself signaled."

Danny leaned closer and brushed his lips across mine. "Message received," he whispered. "Do me a favor and hold next weekend open for us."

I blinked. Surely the vodka float was distorting my abilities to process information. Not an infrequent occurrence. Surely Danny hadn't suggested we wait until next weekend. "Wha-what?" I managed, knowing I looked confused as hell. "What's wrong with tonight?"

Danny's grin turned wicked. "Remember that evening back in May when we stayed up all night talking? Your ground rules. No wine, no liquor. Just food and coffee and talk about the past, Vietnam, and everything in between. Well, my ground rules this time. No wine, no liquor. Just us, and I doubt we'll do as much talking."

I stared into Danny's laughing eyes. *Well, damn. Payback really was a bitch.*

"Besides, one night's not enough for us. We'll need the whole weekend." Then he slid his hand into my hair and pulled my mouth to his. The heat of his kiss burned all vestiges of vodka from my veins. Sober as a judge in an instant.

"Come on, you need to get home, and I

have an early flight tomorrow."

Danny came around to my side of the table and held out his hand. Good thing. After that kiss, I wasn't sure I could walk.

ELEVEN

Friday morning

I clicked out of one of Peter Brewster's rental property spreadsheets and moved to the next in the spreadsheet files. The familiar address at the top was my townhouse. Well, not mine. Peter Brewster had thrown in free rent on his Georgetown property in order to woo me into accepting his job offer last March. It worked. Once I'd seen the lovely two-story brick on P Street with its shady backyard patio, side patio, sunny kitchen, and Jacuzzi in the master suite . . . I was hooked.

I never regretted my decision to move back into the familiar neighborhoods from my days as a Georgetown University student, and from when I was married to my college sweetheart who became a fresh-faced young U.S. Congressman from Colorado after law school. Our two young daughters had played in the playground down the street. Memories were around every corner. But just as there were new children enjoying that playground now, I had decided to make new memories. New life replacing the painful memories of the past.

My personal cell phone's music cut through my wanderings in the past. Early Jefferson Airplane this time. Samantha's name flashed and I clicked on just as Grace Slick's voice rose.

"How're you doing, Miss Thing?" I asked as I relaxed into my leather desk chair. "I'm sure Eleanor's Network has spread the news far and wide."

"I should say," Samantha drawled. "My mice have been calling and texting me since the crack of dawn. I swear the phone woke me up."

"Yay for your mice. I'm sure they're as relieved as I am that you're out of the police spotlight. And the *D.C. Dirt*'s evil eye as well."

"Well, to be honest, half of me is relieved. But the other half is sad dear Bernie is now going to be the subject of that trashy gossip rag."

I couldn't resist. "Hey, Bernie's in his eighties. He'll be flattered. I bet his buddies are calling to congratulate him right now."

She let out a bawdy laugh. "You are so

bad, Molly. God, I love you! You always say exactly what I need to hear."

I took a sip from my newly refilled coffee mug, listening to Samantha's laughter while I pondered bringing up the plan Eleanor and I had discussed the other night. She had given me the perfect opening. Now . . . how to phrase the subject of Samantha Calhoun's rehab?

"You know, Eleanor was worried sick about you, Samantha," I wiggled in sideways. "She hated watching you being dragged through the mud as much as I did."

"She's such a sweet old dear," Samantha's voice gentled. "I'm amazed she hasn't washed her hands of me long ago. I know I've given her fits these last few years."

Another opening . . . I couldn't pass that up. "You're lucky Eleanor's a forgiving sort. In fact, she was so relieved that you would no longer be under suspicion in connection with Wilson's death that she and I came up with a plan. A rehab plan, so to speak." I held my breath, waiting for Samantha's reaction.

There was at least a ten-second pause before she spoke. "*Rehab?* Exactly *what* are you two planning to rehabilitate?" she asked, clearly amused.

Not exactly sure how to phrase it, I simply

plunged in. "Your reputation, Samantha. The Widow Wilson may have opened the door, but there were scores of people who were waiting for an opportunity to drag you down in that mud. Jealousy, resentment, or just plain nastiness. Whatever. You handed them the opportunity when you refused to explain your whereabouts to the police the night of Wilson's death. If you had, this would never have become the scandal it did."

"You're right. As much as it pains me to admit it, I made this horrible event worse by not cooperating with police earlier."

Relieved by her honesty, I continued. "Eleanor said that there were a lot of people who'd envied you your social standing over the years and were waiting gleefully for you to step off that pedestal. Hell, Samantha, you didn't step off, you *jumped* off when you started your congressional dalliances a few years ago."

"You're right about that, sugar," she said with a low laugh.

"It's no laughing matter, Samantha," I chided gently. "Eleanor and I and all your friends hate what's happened to you. That's why Eleanor and I came up with what we think is the perfect way for you to redeem yourself, so to speak. Rehab. Redeem. Re-establish. Whatever you want to call it. Our plan is a little unusual, but it's dramatic. And it'll totally flummox your enemies. Especially the Widow Wilson."

Samantha chuckled. "I can hardly wait to hear the details. I love the idea of flummoxing enemies."

Encouraged, I charged ahead. "Eleanor's offering to take you under her protective wing. You would accompany her to all the charitable functions and social events she attends every week. And they are considerable. You'll be busy seven days and evenings every week. Needless to say, there'll be no time for stray dalliances. Eleanor's Rules, if you will."

"Stray dalliances . . ." she said with a genteel snort.

"I know, I know. You'd be serving a public penance, and that will stick in your craw. But, face it, Miss Thing, it will take something dramatic like that to re-establish yourself in Washington. How better than by Eleanor MacKenzie's side? No one would dare attack you while you're perceived to be under Eleanor's protection. They'd never risk losing favor in Eleanor's eyes, you know that."

"Ah, yes, the Queen Mother would not be pleased."

Sensing that Samantha was considering the idea at least, I continued to pitch. "You would be standing by Eleanor's side, doing good deeds, working with charities. It's a natural. You're already involved with umpteen charities."

"You can stop ladling it on, Molly," she said, laughing. "You've made your point. Yours and Eleanor's."

I sent a brief prayer of thanks heavenward, even though I'd stopped praying years ago. "So, you'll consider it?"

"*Yes,* I'll consider it. No promises, though. God, it would be like joining a convent with Eleanor as the *real* Mother Superior. I don't know if I could do it, Molly. I love my freedom too much."

"Just consider it, okay? That's all I ask. Eleanor doesn't think you'll do it, for the very reasons you mentioned."

"Sharp as ever. You've got to hand it to her. Tell me, when did you two come up with this redemption plan? Was it at Eleanor's charity fundraiser the other day?"

"No, it was last night when she came to one of Senator Russell's senatorial dinners. One of the couples couldn't make it, so Eleanor was kind enough to fill in at the last moment. Peter was her dinner partner, which he thoroughly enjoyed, listening to him talk this morning." A stray memory resurfaced. "By the way, I did meet Natasha Jorgensen at Eleanor's fundraiser. Congresswoman Chertoff had invited two of her staffers to the event with her, and she introduced me to Natasha."

"That was nice of Sally. How'd you like Natasha?"

"She impressed me. Smart, savvy, with a sense of humor. That will help her survive on the Hill. Sally mentioned that the police came to the office and questioned Natasha about Wilson's prescription pill habit. Naturally, I couldn't resist following up on that when I spoke with her alone. Natasha admitted that she'd seen Quentin Wilson with pill bottles on his desk. But when I asked if she knew how long he'd also taken Vicodin, she looked really uncomfortable and acted nervous. She kept glancing away. I didn't let on I knew anything more."

Samantha paused. "I'm sure that's because she didn't want to reveal to police she was the one who gave Quentin that staffer's name. The guy was an old college friend of hers."

"What!"

"I didn't tell you because I didn't want Natasha to get in any trouble. It's not her fault Quentin took too many pills."

"Do you think Natasha lied to the police?"

Samantha released a long sigh. "I was hoping they simply asked about Quentin's pill-taking habit. Natasha's a smart girl, but she's probably afraid the police will try to implicate her. Good Lord! Quentin's death keeps ensnaring people. It's like stepping in quicksand."

I noticed a message from Peter flashing on my computer screen. Time to get back to work. "Well, you can step out of that quicksand with Eleanor's help. Just think about it. Now, I've got to answer this message from Peter. Back to work."

"I promise I'll think about it. And thank you for being such a dear loving friend. I appreciate it, sugar."

There was a trace of the old Samantha's *joie de vivre* in those words. "Anytime, Miss Thing. That's what dear friends are for."

Friday evening

Raymond blew out a long stream of smoke, then spoke into his cell phone. "He's all set up and ready, just waiting for the signal."

"Has Levitz gone out or contacted anyone since he's been there?" Spencer asked.

"No, he's being a good boy, nice and obedient. Following all the instructions Fillmore gave him. He's staying inside his motel room, waiting for Mr. Smith to call." Raymond chuckled softly then took another drag on his cigarette. "He's expecting a new driver's license and the location of a hotel in El Paso where he can stay. Or where he *thinks* he'll be staying."

Spencer laughed softly. "Has our Mr. Smith been keeping him in his sights."

"All the time.

"How's he going to, ah . . . finish it?"

"With the same pill mixture he saved from Wilson. That way there will be a match in dosage. Hypo to the neck. Kid will never know what hit him."

"Good. We want it nice and neat. No loose ends."

"As always. When do you want it done?"

"Tonight. Get it over with, so the news can come out and we can put this Wilson project to bed."

"You got it. Tonight it is."

TWELVE

Monday morning

I turned the pages of the *Washington Post,* aiming for the editorial page, when my eye caught a familiar name headlining a smaller paragraph nestled below the fold on an inner page.

Sylvia Wilson, widow of recently deceased Congressman Quentin Wilson, appointed to late husband's seat in the U.S. House of Representatives.

I smiled and sipped my coffee while I read the official confirmation of the gossip that had buzzed through Washington for over a week. Point for Widow Wilson. Widows had been claiming deceased husbands' congressional seats for nearly a century.

Folding the paper, I went to the kitchen sink and rinsed out my coffee mug. Another beautiful August morning beckoned outside. I grabbed my briefcase and purse and left through the back door in the kitchen. A pungently sweet scent greeted me from the graceful mimosa tree beside the back patio. Laden with delicate pink blossoms, the sweet perfume engulfed me as I walked toward the front yard and sidewalk.

Bruce lay stretched out in his customary morning sunny spot on the bricks edging the upper flower bed. Like many Georgetown townhomes, the front yard sloped up so the gardens were tiered to accommodate the narrow frontage.

"Stay away from the birds, Bruce," I called in my customary admonition. Bruce simply meowed and smiled his inscrutable kitty smile.

I was leaving a few minutes earlier than usual so I could finally make a phone call that had been niggling in the back of my mind for days, ever since I'd spoken with Natasha Jorgensen at Eleanor's fundraiser. Natasha had e-mailed me the name of a senior researcher that Quentin Wilson had used. Loretta Wade. Now that worries about Samantha no longer took my concentration, I could afford to indulge my curiosity.

Considering the story Samantha had told me about Wilson's eavesdropping experience and his subsequent research into financial legislation, I was curious what Wilson was looking for. Samantha said he seemed "obsessed" with the topics. I wondered if this Loretta Wade might know more. Slipping my cell phone from my purse, I paged through the directory where I'd entered Loretta Wade's name and office number at the Congressional Research Service. I clicked on her name and listened to the phone ring, finally changing to voice mail. Loretta Wade's voice came on and announced that she'd return my call as soon as possible. I'd detected a note of "no nonsense" to Loretta Wade's tone that I liked. After the beep I left a brief message identifying myself as a member of Senator Russell's staff calling in reference to a research question, then left my number and clicked off. I sensed Loretta Wade didn't like to waste time.

I spied Casey leaving the Russell kitchen, coffee mug in hand. "Did you leave me any, Casey?" I teased as I approached. Midmorning e-mails were vying with financial spreadsheets for my attention. Switching between them demanded more caffeine than usual.

"Don't worry, Molly. There's plenty left. Luisa just made a fresh pot," Casey said with a big smile.

"Exactly what I need." I headed straight

for the coffeepot. "Spreadsheet columns are starting to blend into one another. That's a sign of severe caffeine deprivation."

Casey leaned against the doorway. "I see the Widow Wilson has been appointed to her husband's seat. You were spot on, Molly," he said then sipped his coffee.

I watched that beautiful black stream splash into my oversized mug. "It wasn't my prediction. It was Samantha's. She's the sage of Washington politics, not me."

"Sage of Washington politics," Casey said with a chuckle. "At least she's no longer in the Fairfax County cops' spotlight. That's the important thing. I have a feeling Samantha Calhoun can handle the *D.C. Dirt*'s spotlight. By the way, have you seen it yet today? I thought you'd get a kick out of their announcement of Sylvia Wilson's appointment." He reached inside his jacket and retrieved the slender newssheet and handed it over.

"Ahhhh, gossip and caffeine, perfect combination," I said, then took a big sip. "Please tell me Samantha's not in here."

"Nope. Not a word. But you will enjoy the Widow Wilson gossip. Looks like they've been digging around."

Casey had conveniently folded the news rag right at the article about Sylvia Wilson.

"Good. It's about time Widow Wilson got a dose of her own medicine." I scanned the columns, recognizing the same information I'd heard from both Samantha and Natasha Jorgensen. Years of campaign donations to the Ohio Governor, rude and overbearing with Wilson's congressional staffers, old Ohio family, father a wealthy Cleveland real estate developer, and much, much more. I couldn't help smiling while I read.

"Well, well, looks like the *Dirt*'s found all those disgruntled Quentin Wilson staffers. I hate to admit this, but I'm glad. After the way she went after Samantha, I hope the *Dirt* makes Sylvia Wilson's life hell."

"Welcome to Washington, Widow Wilson," Casey said with a grin, reaching inside his jacket for his ringing cell phone as he stepped into the hall.

I sipped my steaming coffee and headed back to my office and the waiting spreadsheets, while I debated calling Samantha so we could gloat over the phone together. Clicking my screen to life once more, I was about to dive back into a rental property income statement when my own personal phone rang. It had to be Samantha, I figured and got ready to gloat.

"Molly Malone," I answered, expecting to hear Samantha's amused drawl. Instead, I heard the same no-nonsense voice from earlier this morning.

"Ms. Malone, this is Loretta Wade. I'm returning your call about a research subject Senator Russell is interested in."

"Oh, yes, yes, Ms. Wade," I quickly switched gears. "I wanted to talk with you about some . . . some research topics. I'd like to explain more. When would be the best time we could talk?"

"Well, we're talking right now, Ms. Malone. What is it that Senator Russell is interested in researching? He's already on the Senate Energy and Natural Resources Committee, subcommittee on Energy. And I know he's recently been appointed to the Banking, Housing, and Urban Affairs Committee."

I hesitated, wondering how to explain to "no-nonsense" Loretta Wade that the research was for me and not Senator Russell. My plan was to invite Loretta Wade to lunch so I could explain face-to-face. Over the phone, I was afraid my request would sound weird at best, suspicious at worst.

"I can actually better explain what I'm looking for in person. I thought maybe I could meet you for lunch?"

Loretta Wade paused for a split second. "Excuse me?"

From the sound of Ms. Wade's tone, I knew my suggestion had come across way more than weird. "I know it may sound strange, but it's hard to explain over the phone —"

"Ms. Malone, I'm a busy woman. I've got a large staff to oversee and research requests waiting this minute. I take lunch at my desk and do not do business dinners. I don't have the time. So, you need to explain exactly what you want to research to me on the phone now."

Oh, brother. I figured I'd better think fast or Loretta Wade would hang up on me. I took a quick breath and plunged in. "The questions relate to Congressman Quentin Wilson's recent research requests into financial legislation. I was curious what he had learned because . . . because my late niece, Karen Grayson, was doing similar research before she died. I'm . . . trying to finish her work. Kind of like a tribute to her, I suppose."

I held my breath, hoping I'd struck a sympathetic chord somewhere inside no-nonsense Loretta. I hadn't heard a click on the other end, so I knew she was still there, not saying anything. I ventured again. "I know it sounds weird or maybe even stupid . . ."

"No, it doesn't, Ms. Malone," Loretta Wade's voice came. The brusque business tone was softened now, around the edges. "I knew your niece, Karen. She was a fine young woman, and I was sickened by what happened to her."

Taken by surprise by the feeling behind her words, I paused for a heartbeat. "So was I. And thank you for saying that, Ms. Wade. It means a lot." My instinct said to stop talking. Most of the time I failed to obey that admonition, but I did this time.

A big sigh came over the phone. "All right, Ms. Malone. Let me look at my calendar."

I couldn't believe it. My appeal for sympathy worked. By invoking my beloved niece's name, I'd been able to establish some level of credibility with no-nonsense Loretta Wade.

"I still have one teenager at home, so my evenings are usually full. Let's see . . . how about Wednesday night? My son is at tennis practice. I can squeeze in dinner then."

"That's great, Ms. Wade. Thank you so much."

"It would be easier for me if we met somewhere closer to my house, so I can be home when he returns. I'm over in the Eastern Market area. You know where that is, don't you?"

"Sure I do." I'd already gone wandering through Eastern Market's great Saturday morning market earlier this summer.

"Good. There's a tavern-style restaurant on the Eastern Market side of Eighth Street. Why don't we meet there, say six thirty?"

"That's perfect. Thanks so much for taking time away from your busy schedule. I remember how hectic that was, getting my two daughters to and from practices and lessons. They're all grown now."

"Well, my other two sons are grown but Tommy's the baby. Once he gets into college I can relax."

Surprised by her honest and open statement, I laughed softly. "I know what you mean. Hang in there, Loretta, the finish line is in sight. Okay if I call you that? I'm a first-name person by nature."

"Sure thing, Molly. Right now, both of us should get back to work. I'll see you Wednesday night."

"I'll put it on my daytimer, Loretta." Somehow I got the feeling I was going to really enjoy Wednesday night's supper.

Monday evening
Rinsing a bunch of fresh spinach under my kitchen faucet, I grabbed some paper towels. Halfway paying attention to the D.C. metro-

area news broadcast coming from the small television on the edge of the counter, I patted the spinach dry and chose a handful to add to the fresh tomatoes, onions, peppers, and mushrooms I'd chopped. Summer's harvest did not disappoint. My mouth was watering at the sight of those juicy red tomatoes.

I'd already eaten a small one. Couldn't resist. It was in my mouth before I knew it.

I tossed the salad ingredients into one of my larger salad bowls. What wasn't consumed tonight would be lunch tomorrow. The TV newscaster was describing all the traffic jams clogging roads from the District into Maryland and Virginia. Giving thanks once again that I didn't have to sit in rush hour traffic every day, I was surprised by the man's sudden change of subject.

"Breaking news. We've just received word that the body of a young male found in Houston, Texas, over the weekend may be the missing congressional staffer who was connected to the recently deceased Congressman Quentin Wilson." I stared at the television as the news reporter wearing a suit talked into the camera. "Apparently, the cause of death of the young man found in Texas was a large overdose of sleeping pills and prescription drugs. If viewers will recall, Congressman Wilson also died from an apparent overdose of sleeping pills and prescription painkillers. It was rumored that Congressman Wilson had obtained the drugs from a staffer who worked for Congressional Research Service on Capitol Hill. Police are not releasing the name of the deceased, pending notification of his family."

The news reporter's voice and demeanor changed from sharp and reportorial to warm and folksy as he announced a pancake breakfast for a local charity group next weekend.

That had to be the same guy Samantha mentioned. *Good Lord!* Samantha was right. Wilson's death had become like quicksand. It kept sucking people in.

I left the salad bowl on the counter and reached for my cell phone, skimming through my directory until I found Samantha's name. She answered after three rings.

"I knew that was you calling, Molly," she said. "Yes, I just saw the news broadcast about the young staffer."

"I figure it's gotta be the same guy we saw on your video. If police are releasing the information to the media, that means they've already identified the body."

"Sad to say, I think you're right. It's

simply awful how the ripples keep appearing from Quentin's death. Tragic. Somewhere this young man had a mother and father and family that loved him."

"I wonder how Natasha Jorgensen is taking it."

"Probably not well, especially if they were close. I wonder what he was doing in Texas?"

"Maybe he heard that police had learned of his delivery business and came to ask him questions. I'll bet he panicked and headed out of town."

"This is all so sad . . ." Her voice trailed off.

"You'd better continue to keep your head down, Samantha. You haven't been mentioned in the sleaze rag for a couple of days. But this news will stir up all those stories again. So lie low."

"Oh, I am. I'm keeping out of sight. My friends are coming here to visit. By the way, I'd love to have you for dinner, unless Danny has made you a better offer. I hope he has."

I paused before telling Samantha how my last date with Danny had ended. "Danny's out of town until Friday. But he asked me to reserve this weekend for us. The entire weekend. He said we'd need it."

Samantha let out a jubilant hoot. "Thank Gawd! *Finally!* I was about to come over and knock both your heads together and tell you to get on with it. You two were giving *me* a headache."

I laughed softly. "I figured you'd be pleased. I also think you'll get a kick out of Danny's rules for the weekend."

"Rules? Something kinky, I hope? I'll have my lingerie shop send over something appropriate. Now, tell me. What are 'the rules'?"

"Very simple, actually. No wine, no liquor. Just us."

Samantha laughed so hard, I had to hold the phone away from my ear. Meanwhile, I snitched a chunk of juicy tomato and popped it into my mouth. *Delicious.*

"On the evening newscast. Perfect," Spencer's deep voice sounded over the phone.

"Yeah, I thought so. The kid's wallet and ID were right there. Houston cops couldn't miss it. I figured it would take until today for the local cops to pick up on it. They were already looking for him."

"Yes, Larry Fillmore called and told me he'd heard various staffers were questioned last week, so police already knew Levitz left town."

Raymond took another drag on his cigarette as he slowed his pace down K Street. *Damn!* He couldn't even talk and walk at the same time anymore. He veered from the sidewalk into Farragut Square's small park on the corner at 17th and K Street. "Things will start to die down now. Wilson is dead and buried. Widow Wilson has taken over his seat. And the sleazy staffer who sold drugs on the side has taken the same poison he was delivering. Nice and tidy ending."

"Let's hope. I told Larry to start leaking info about photos of Wilson and Calhoun to his *D.C. Dirt* source. Let the press start to speculate about it. Were they blackmail photos? Then, drop hints about Wilson's widow. Gradually build suspicion that she was going to use the photos in a divorce. That ought to put the matter to rest. Logical conclusion that Wilson ended it all after learning about his wife's plan to divorce him and use the photos."

Raymond chuckled. "Sounds good. I'll give my guy at the *Post* a heads up. Maybe he'll bite. See if we can get some mainstream coverage on that. At the least, it'll be fun to watch the Widow Wilson squirm." Raymond relaxed against the green bench and laughed. Spencer's laughter already echoed across the phone.

Thirteen

Tuesday

I switched songs on my iPod as I leaned against the stone bridge wall on 31st Street that arched over the C&O Canal. The canal ran parallel between Georgetown's main drag, M Street, and the Potomac River only two blocks away. I checked my watch again: 5:35 a.m. Early enough so not many cars drove past me on the bridge. High-rise office buildings and condo apartments lined most of the two blocks between me and the river. Riverfront views were as gorgeous as they were pricey.

But I didn't even bother looking toward the river; my attention was fixed on the towpath, the half-dirt, half-paved trail that bordered the canal. Barge-pulling mules once trod that path three hundred years ago. Now, runners and tourists used the path, which ran all the way to Great Falls in Virginia.

It was a perfect early August morning — before the heat rose and there was only a whisper of humidity. Since I'd forced myself to get up an hour earlier than usual, I knew I should really take advantage of this gorgeous weather and start my morning run. Instead, I stood waiting and watching. Watching for tall, slender, blond Natasha Jorgensen to come striding along. She'd told me she ran along the canal every morning between Rock Creek Parkway and Key Bridge, starting at five thirty. Surely, I hadn't missed her. I'd gotten to my 31st Street stone bridge perch by five fifteen.

I peered down the stretch of canal towpath that led from the parkway, searching for signs of a woman running. I'd seen several runners since I'd arrived, but they were all men. All except a lone slender gray-haired woman, and I doubted young Natasha had suddenly decided to go gray.

Then, my eyes picked up a speck behind the overhanging trees. I waited, and sure enough, the figure of a woman appeared, running along the towpath. I yanked out the earbuds and shoved my little music player into my pocket as I headed from the bridge down to the towpath along the canal. The runner was tall, blond, and slender, so I gambled it was Natasha and waited for her to pass me to confirm.

A scant two minutes later, Natasha Jorgensen passed by and I set off in her wake, picking up my pace. I called out, "Hey, Natasha!"

Natasha jerked around and stared at me, wide-eyed, clearly startled. I waved and smiled as I closed the distance, and I watched a look of recognition flash over her face.

"Hey, Molly!" she said as I pulled beside her.

"Sorry. Didn't mean to startle you," I said, matching her stride. "I remember you said you ran really early here, so I thought I'd give it a try. Escape the summer heat, you know?" Thanks to my regular running with Danny, my stamina had increased these last four months so I could run at a good pace and talk without losing my breath.

"I love it early like this," Natasha said, glancing around. "It's so pretty and you can really hear the birds without so many cars driving up above." She pointed to the main thoroughfare of M Street above.

"I hope I'm not disturbing you," I ventured. "Some people don't like to talk while they run."

Natasha shook her head. "Naw. It's okay. I was just going through a lot of stuff in my head. There's a lot going on."

I spotted another runner up ahead, coming our way. Sweating, T-shirt stuck to his chest. Notre Dame. Another runner right behind. Buzzed haircut said military. More runners would appear. Early morning was prime time to run before tackling rush hour traffic. Meanwhile, I figured I'd better ask the question I'd gotten up so early for. If I could find a way to ease into it.

"You know, there's another reason I decided to run early today. There's something I wanted to ask you, Natasha. You know that gossip in the *D.C. Dirt* about the Hill staffer supplying pills to people? Samantha said Quentin Wilson told her you had a friend who could get him pills. Was that the same guy?"

Natasha immediately lowered her head, staring at the ground as we ran rather than at the trail ahead. After a few seconds her quiet voice answered. "Yes, it was. Congressman Wilson looked so haggard and jumpy a few months ago, and he was starting to snap at people. I was worried about him. So, I told him about this guy I know, a friend from college, who worked over at Congressional Research Service."

Natasha went quiet while we ran past the balcony of the café restaurant where Danny and I had lunch the day he first walked back into my life. The café was empty now. Too early for customers. I deliberately matched my stride to Natasha's so we would be in rhythm. Meanwhile, I chose my next words carefully.

"I don't know if you saw the local TV news last night, but it sounds like the young man they found dead in Houston is that same guy. This morning's news said his name was Gary Levitz, and they mentioned he worked on Capitol Hill."

Natasha didn't answer right away, so we strode together in silence along the towpath, only the sound of our sneakers hitting the dirt path. Key Bridge lay up ahead, its shadowed underpass arching over the towpath and canal. My radar always went on alert whenever I ran beneath that huge bridge that stretched from Virginia across the Potomac River and the canal before emptying into Georgetown's M Street. Danny had warned me to be careful if I ran there alone. During the summer, drunks and vagrants would sleep off the previous night's binge beneath that protective concrete arch.

"Yes, I saw the news last night," Natasha finally spoke. "And I knew it was Gary. I just knew it. It's so awful. First, Congressman Wilson. Now Gary. All because of those stupid pills!"

"I'm sorry you lost your friend, Natasha. Had you known him long?"

She wiped her hand beneath her nose as we neared the underpass. "I'd gone to school with him back at the University of Minnesota. We dated a few times. And we both came to the Hill the same year. Gary was a smart guy, and he never did any drugs that I know of in college. So I was really surprised when he told me what he was doing now. But Gary insisted his uncle was a doctor, and it was okay to fill extra prescriptions. So I told myself it was okay. I mean, his uncle was a *doctor,* after all. Surely, it would be all right." She went silent for several long strides. "But it wasn't. And the Congressman is dead. And now Gary is dead. Part of me still feels guilty. I should never have told Congressman Wilson about Gary."

"Don't do that to yourself, Natasha," I consoled as we approached the underpass. "You were trying to help the Congressman. Quentin Wilson chose to take those pills that night. We'll never know if he did it deliberately or accidentally. Who knows what was going on in his mind? I think the police said he was drinking, so that had to cloud his judgment."

My words echoed as we ran beneath the concrete span. The low rumble of tires vibrated on the asphalt above our heads, reverberating around us and side to side. I peered into the darker crevices beneath the span as we passed. No vagrants to be seen, just the distinct odor of urine rising in the early morning air to greet us.

"Maybe I couldn't have stopped Congressman Wilson, but I might have been able to stop Gary." An anxious tone captured her voice now. "When police first questioned me at Chertoff's office, they asked if I knew anything about Wilson's Vicodin prescriptions. I told them I'd seen pill bottles on his desk. That's all. I admit I was scared. I didn't want police to think I was involved in Gary's business. But now I'm feeling guilty. If I'd told police what Gary was doing, then he wouldn't have gone running off to Texas. He'd be in trouble with the police, but Gary would still be alive!"

"You don't know that, Natasha. Gary knew exactly when the police started asking questions. You know how stuff spreads all over the Hill. No way were you the only one who knew about his side business. I'll bet Gary got texts the minute the detectives showed up on Capitol Hill. He probably took off for Texas the moment word spread."

Natasha was silent as we strode along the canal, traffic noise of M Street getting louder and closer. "This is where I like to turn," she said.

We slowed our strides and turned around to return the way we came. Traffic had increased on Key Bridge in the scant few minutes since we'd first passed beneath. Suddenly, something Natasha had said a moment ago came back into my mind.

"I'm assuming Gary had a car," I asked, edging into my question.

"Yes. He'd just bought a new one. A Mazda. Really pretty. Bright blue."

"Boy, Texas is a long drive from Washington."

"He didn't drive. He told me he flew to Dallas, then took a bus somewhere else."

My little buzzer went off. "So you must have talked to him after he got to Texas."

"Yes. He called me after he got there. He wouldn't tell me where he was, just some motel. I told him to be careful and stay in touch."

"Why'd he take a plane then a bus? Did he run out of money or something?" I probed.

"You know, I asked him that. He said he couldn't use his car, but he didn't explain why. Just said he needed to fly into Dallas, then take a bus and pay cash for everything."

The word "needed" flashed in my mind. "That's kind of weird. I wonder if he was meeting someone there?" I conjectured out loud. "Did he mention anyone?"

"Not exactly. But I got the feeling he was. When I asked how long he would be there, he said probably only a couple of days. He'd be moving someplace else as soon as he got a new ID. Of course, that really worried me."

Hmmmm. I pondered as we returned beneath the underpass. This time, another runner passed us by. Probably military from the look of him.

"A new ID, huh? Sounds like Gary might have been making a run for the border. Or, maybe simply start working some job with his new identity. There're a lot of big cities in Texas, and they're spread out. Lots of little towns surrounding them where he could blend in. A lot easier than in Mexico."

"Oh, I wish he had! Maybe he'd still be alive and safe."

"And maybe not. It sounds like Gary had more problems bedeviling him than you knew. Otherwise, he wouldn't have taken his own life."

We strode past the Park Service barge

used to give tourists a ride down the Canal in good weather. The sun was beginning its morning climb. I could feel the temperature and humidity rise together — in tandem.

"Oh, Gary . . . why did you do it?" Natasha asked sadly.

"We'll never know. None of us really knows what's going on inside another person's head, even if they're a loved one. My husband killed himself years ago during his third term. He was brilliant and passionate and cared so much for the people he represented in Colorado. Yet . . . he shot himself. After all these years, I still haven't figured out why. Why would he end his life like that? I have no answers. The reasons died with him."

Natasha glanced at me as we approached the next access point to the connecting streets. "I'd heard about that, Molly. I'm sorry."

"Keep the good memories of Gary," I advised, not allowing myself to dwell with those sad memories from the past. They had a power of their own. "That's what I did, and I kept Dave alive for his daughters. Listen, I'm going to head back to my house so I can get ready for the office. Take care, Natasha, and let's stay in touch, okay?"

"I will. And thanks." Natasha gave me a

little smile before I turned off the towpath and headed toward Wisconsin Avenue and the streets above.

"Good morning, Molly," Luisa greeted. "There's a beautiful surprise waiting in your office. From the colonel." She gave me that Cheshire cat smile of hers.

I had to laugh as I walked down the hallway toward my office. "Danny is retired from the Marines, Luisa. So, he's no longer a colonel. Technically."

Luisa gave a dismissive wave as she walked beside me. "Once a colonel, always a colonel. That's what I say."

It was hard to argue with reasoning like that, so I switched subjects. "How're those grandbabies of yours doing?"

"Getting bigger by the day," Luisa beamed. "I've got more pictures I'll show you later. But right now, you'd best get to your office. There was a note attached to your gift, so I imagine you'll want to answer it. Oh, and I brought you a mug of coffee, so you won't be interrupted."

I grinned at Luisa the Matchmaker. "Thanks, Luisa, you're a sweetheart. I'll read that note right away. And I'll send Danny your regards."

Luisa simply grinned conspiratorially

before she headed toward the upstairs stairway.

Sure enough, there was a vase of brilliant summer roses in the middle of my desk. Crimson red, coral pink, snow white, and sunshine yellow rimmed with red. Gorgeous. I settled into my desk chair and opened the small white envelope taped to the vase. The handwritten message was short.

"Thinking of you. Love, Danny."

I read those five words and felt their message work through me. And their meaning.

Oh, God . . . the "L" word. Now what?

I experienced a brief flush of anxiety sweep over me. Neither Danny nor I had ever used the word. Not with each other. Now Danny had done it. Served the ball into my court. Thrown down the gauntlet. *Crap. Now what?*

I stared at the little card, the words taunting me. *This is a test. I know it is.* Danny said it first just to see what I'd do. Sneaky. What could you expect from someone who'd spent years creeping around jungles, deserts, whatever. I put the card beside my cell phone and picked up my coffee, hoping the caffeine would settle my thoughts.

No such luck. All it did was allow the two

competing Voices Inside My Head to have at it.

For God's sake! What are you agonizing about, woman? Crazy Ass insisted. *Of course, you love him!*

Not so fast! Sober-and-Righteous cautioned. *There's no need to attach more importance to this relationship than it warrants. It's merely a primal mating ritual. Hormones, glands, what-have-you.*

Don't be ridiculous. You know it's more than that. Just text the man that you love him. How hard is that?

Hold on! Do not confuse sexual attraction with love.

You've got to be kidding, Crazy Ass countered. *Pick up the phone and send him a text. The weekend is fast approaching.*

Sober mumbled something incoherent, so I stared at the card as it sat there, accusing me. Waiting for me to answer. *Return Danny's serve. Pick up the gauntlet.*

What is it with these sports metaphors?

I ignored Crazy Ass, and picked up my phone. Finding Danny's name in the directory, I keyed in a simple text. "The flowers are beautiful. I love them. Thank you so much." I hesitated over the send button, then pressed it.

Steady on, Sober decreed, obviously pleased with my cowardly decision, while Crazy Ass made all sorts of clucking chicken noises. I tried to ignore them both by turning my attention to a copy of the *D.C. Dirt* in the middle of my desk. Casey had drawn an arrow to a short paragraph above the fold in the "Whispers and Rumors" section.

Sources close to the *Dirt* have let us know that photographs taken of recently departed Congressman Quentin Wilson and his paramour have surfaced. Apparently, these photos show the congressman and his lover *in flagrante delicto.* The *Dirt* cannot help but wonder: who would take such photos? Was someone blackmailing Congressman Wilson? Was that why he took an overdose of sleeping pills and painkillers? The *Dirt* wants to know.

I stared at the paragraph. *Oh, no. Not the photos.* I grabbed for my phone again and punched in Samantha's number. She answered on the third ring.

"Hello, Molly, I take it you've read the morning sleaze rag."

"Good Lord, Samantha, I'm so sorry. How in the world did they learn about the photos? It had to be a leak at the police department, don't you think?"

"I haven't a clue," she said, her voice sounding tired. "But my lawyer has already delivered a letter advising that rag we will sue them up one side and down the other if they print that trash."

"Do you think that will work?"

She let out a long sigh. "I have no idea. But it's the only thing we can do at this point. Threaten to sue the bejeezus out of them."

"I'm so sorry, Samantha." I vainly searched for something else to say and remembered my morning run. "Let's change the subject. I took my morning run by the C&O Canal and saw Natasha Jorgensen so we ran together for a while. She confirmed that the guy in Texas was her staffer friend, Gary Levitz."

"You and I figured as much. Listen, Molly . . . I've done a lot of thinking this morning, and I'd like you to call Eleanor and tell her that I gratefully accept her offer of shelter from the storm. I thought the clouds were lifting, but after this news, I can tell that a tempest is brewing. I welcome Eleanor's kind offer. Joining the convent, so to speak."

I heard a hint of Samantha's old self surfacing. "You'll survive. Meanwhile, any innuendo the *Dirt* throws your way won't stick. You'll be out there doing good deeds. What is it the nuns used to say . . . doing charitable work?"

"Good Lord, don't remind me. This may kill me, you know."

"Celibacy never killed anyone, Samantha."

"Spoken by a woman who's about to spend the entire weekend *in flagrante delicto,*" she drawled the words. "Mad, wild sex."

Oh, yeah! Crazy Ass cheered. Sober simply scowled.

I just laughed. "By the way, thanks for the lingerie. The shop delivered the box yesterday. Gorgeous, simply gorgeous. Almost as pretty as the flowers Danny sent this morning."

"Ohhhhh, good. He sent flowers. Smart man."

I hesitated, then said, "And a card saying 'Thinking of you. *Love,* Danny.' "

Samantha paused for a moment. "Tell me you replied in kind, Molly. Or I'm gonna come over there and smack you."

That made me laugh. "Yes, yes, I did . . . I thanked him for the flowers."

"And?"

"And that was it. I chickened out with the L word."

"Molleeeee . . . what am I gonna do with you? You know you love him and he loves you. Now stop acting like a jackass!"

"Why can't we just have sex? Why do we have to talk about love? Isn't there a song about that? What's love got —"

"God, Molly, you're impossible, you know that?"

"I can't help it. It's my nature," I deliberately teased, hoping my lighter tone would deflect her aim.

Not in the least. "You're just afraid of commitment, Molly. Committing yourself."

That shook me. *What the hell?* "I am not! Don't be ridiculous! I was married twice. I loved Dave and . . ."

"You loved Dave and were *committed* to helping his career. Helping him become the man you saw inside him. And then he died before he could live up to your expectations. And, Frank, hell, I saw the two of you together. You were old friends from the Denver political arena. You two made a good team. You were *committed* to working together. But admit it, Molly. You didn't love Frank."

Whoa . . . Samantha's aim was as true as ever. Right straight to the bull's-eye.

"You know I'm right. But Danny is something else again. This man moves you. I can see it. You admitted it a couple of weeks ago. You said he reached something inside you. And that was scary. Because this time, you'd be committing *yourself.*"

I considered what she'd said for a long minute. "You're right. It does scare me."

"Look, I understand because it's happened to me. I didn't want to admit how much Quentin had gotten to me. The real me. I loved him. That's why all this hurts so much. But you and Danny have each other right now. We don't get that many chances in life. Don't let this slip away. You'll regret it. Trust me."

Samantha's words resonated. She was right, as always. "I promise. I won't let it slip away, Miss Thing. Thanks for the advice. And the sexy lingerie."

"Anytime, sugar," she lapsed into her old drawl. "It'll be easier for me to take the vows under Mother Superior MacKenzie if I know you and Danny are enjoying each other. At least one of us will be having fun."

I laughed out loud, the image of Samantha in a habit traipsing after Eleanor. "We'll do our best." The sound of my cell beeping caught my attention. "Uh, oh. There's a text. I bet it's Danny."

"Well, hang up and answer it, sugar. Stop

wasting time. Talk to you later." She clicked off.

Sure enough, the blinking green light on my phone indicated a text waiting. From Danny. Like the first message, it was short.

"Glad you liked the flowers. How about the note?"

Damn! That man was positively spooky. I paused over the keypad then entered the words: "Love you too." Then hit Send.

I picked up my coffee and drained the mug, then turned on my computer. Work was waiting. I was about to go for a coffee refill before I settled into the financial accounts when I heard the telltale beep from my phone. I stared at the blinking green light, then pushed it. Another message from Danny.

"See? That wasn't so hard. It'll get easier. I promise."

This time I laughed out loud. Reading my mind or not, I had to love a man like that. And this time, I meant it.

Raymond signaled the waitress for more coffee as the man he was waiting for slipped into the seat across from him in the booth. The sports bar was only halfway full at mid-afternoon. A major league baseball game was playing on the large screen over the bar.

New York versus Baltimore. The Yankees were ahead.

"Coffee, sir?" the waitress asked the sandy-haired man.

The man smiled warmly at the woman. "No, thank you, ma'am. I'll take a Sam Adams instead."

Raymond loved to watch him work that charm, that warm and folksy manner. No wonder he was always able to get close to every target. He was the guy next door. Wide face, easy smile, relaxed, laid-back manner. The guy at the bar that you'd joke with, share a beer with, and watch the football game on the television above. A woman wouldn't hesitate asking this guy for help if her car broke down. No hesitation whatsoever, unless . . . she looked into his eyes. Ice blue. Even on a hot, humid August afternoon.

Raymond wiped his no-longer-white handkerchief across his forehead and took a sip of the steaming black coffee. The man facing him smiled, just a little.

"You know, you wouldn't sweat so much if you didn't drink that stuff," he said, pointing to the coffee cup. "It's August, in case you hadn't noticed."

"Helps when I'm inside and can't smoke," Raymond admitted and picked up one of the paper-wrapped lozenges lying on the table. "Along with these."

Something that could have passed for concern flickered briefly across the man's wide face, then was gone. "You should have that looked at. Sounds worse."

Raymond shrugged. He already knew it was. Instead, he lied. "I did. It's about the same. So, what's so important you wanted to see me? The Texas job went smooth as silk. You didn't drive all the way out here to Fairfax to have a beer. What's up?"

"I copied the kid's cell phone logs before I left the motel room. Once I got to my computer I downloaded the numbers he called after he left D.C. A couple of calls to Fillmore's decoy phone, one call to his parents, his call to my decoy phone, and one call to a D.C. number. That was the longest call, and it was the night he arrived in Houston. I ran a check and the number belongs to Natasha Jorgensen, who used to be Quentin Wilson's chief of staff."

Raymond looked up over his coffee. *Damn!* He hadn't expected that. "What the hell? Why'd he call her? Is she still over in Wilson's office, working for his wife?"

The man shook his head. "Nope. She ran for the exit like most of that staff. Jorgensen now works as a regular staffer for Congresswoman Sally Chertoff. Like you, I was curious about their connection, so I ran a check on Jorgensen. Seems she and Levitz went to the University of Minnesota together. Were friends with benefits. In fact, she helped him land a job in D.C. after she started working on the Hill eight years ago."

Raymond scowled. "*Dammit!* Now, I'm wondering what Levitz told her that night. Fillmore warned him not to talk with anyone. Told him he had to make a clean break. No contacts. Stupid kid!" He popped another lozenge into his mouth.

"I wondered about that too. So I took the liberty of starting surveillance on Jorgensen. Started yesterday after she left the Hill. I wanted to let you know now, so you could check with the higher-ups. See how they want to move forward."

"Smart move, Trask. I'll check with Spencer, but I'm sure he'll want her home computer checked. Meanwhile, stay on her. See who she talks to."

"Roger that." Trask reached inside his shirt pocket and pulled out a key-ring-sized computer storage device. "Meanwhile, you might want to take a look at this. I followed Jorgensen on her early morning run. I was camped out in front of her apartment on Virginia Avenue, so I wouldn't miss her leaving for the Hill. Instead, she ran out of the building at five in the morning and headed for the C&O Canal to run along the towpath."

"Bloody early if you ask me," Raymond said, then took a deep drink of coffee. The hot liquid felt good on his throat. He popped another lozenge into his mouth.

"She started running alone then a woman joined her. I followed a safe distance behind. They ran together quite awhile, past the bridge, then turned around and came back. The other woman took off for M Street, but I got a good look at her when I ran past them." He paused.

Raymond took another sip, then looked over his cup at his colleague. "And? Did you recognize her?"

Trask gave a small smile. "Oh, yeah. It's that Malone woman. The one Spencer said to check on last spring for a couple of weeks. We never picked up anything unusual, so Spencer told us to stop. No need to bother with her anymore."

Raymond stared into the ice blue eyes looking into his. *Dammit to hell,* he said softly. "Not good. Not good at all."

"I figured that would get your attention . . . and Spencer's. Naturally, I ran a check on Malone to see what connection there was with Jorgensen. Didn't find any. But I did find a ton of stuff connecting Malone with Wilson's girlfriend, Samantha Calhoun. Seems she and Malone knew each other as teenagers when their fathers were both U.S. Senators here in D.C. There's lots of stuff here. You'll enjoy it." He handed the flash drive to Raymond.

"Son of a bitch," Raymond muttered, shaking his head. "I had a feeling about that Malone woman last spring. I don't like loose ends. And just when we had everything all tied up with Wilson, nice and neat. *Damn."*

"Look at it this way. It keeps us in business," Trask said with an engaging smile.

Raymond started to laugh, until the cough started. And didn't stop. Trask signaled the waitress for more coffee.

FOURTEEN

Wednesday morning

Casey leaned inside the Russell kitchen, coffee in one hand, copy of the *D.C. Dirt* in the other. "You are really gonna enjoy this," he said, grinning at me as he waved the paper.

I watched the stream of coffee pouring into my cup. "Don't tell me. Widow Wilson again. What's she up to now?"

"I don't want to spoil your fun. Besides, I've gotta pick up Peter and the Senator. Don't forget, another reception tonight." He dropped the news rag on the counter beside the doorway. "I'll be back before the caterers show up," he called as he headed down the hall.

I took a small sip of the steaming black potion. Hot, hot.

Picking up the *D.C. Dirt,* my eyes immediately found the article that Casey had starred with his red pen. I scanned it as I walked back to my office. Only one paragraph. But oh, what was packed into those few sentences.

No evidence of a blackmail message accompanied photos sent to Congressman Wilson and his paramour. Why, then, were photos taken? And why does Sylvia Wilson have copies of the photos? Did she pay a detective to spy on her cheating husband? Did she threaten to use those photos against him in a divorce? Without Sylvia Wilson's family money, Congressman Wilson would have had difficulty running for re-election next year. Did Sylvia Wilson's threats drive her husband to suicide? Widow Wilson has stepped smoothly into the vacancy her husband's death created. Sources tell the *Dirt* Sylvia Wilson has always expressed an interest in politics.

I couldn't help smiling as I rounded the corner into my office. It looked like the Widow Wilson was beginning to reap what she had sown. If you live by the sword, you die by the sword. Gossip in Washington was far more effective a weapon than burnished steel. More politicians had lost their "political" lives to gossip and innuendo. In the end, they might still be alive but were seriously weakened. Words were powerful.

My computer screen was buzzing with flashing e-mails, indicating new messages. I settled into my chair and grabbed my personal phone, then sent a short text to Samantha.

"Well, we've seen her dish it out. Let's see if Sylvia Wilson can take it."

By the time I'd scrolled through my on-screen e-mails, deciding on which to answer first, Samantha had texted her reply.

"Washington ain't Cleveland, sugar."

I laughed out loud. *Not by a long shot.*

Raymond settled into the cushioned lawn chair on his shaded backyard patio. Cicadas buzzed in the afternoon heat. No views of cranes or construction back here, just oak trees, elms, and maples edging his back fence, stretching as far as he could see.

He'd hoped he'd be safe from encroaching sprawl when he left Fairfax County several years ago and moved to adjoining Prince William County. It only took two years for the bulldozers to appear. How long before the trees would be decimated and thinned, as Caterpillars carved out another subdivision?

His cell phone rang into life on the glass table by his elbow. He took a big sip of brandy before answering. He knew who it was. *Spencer.* "What did you hear from Fillmore?" he asked in greeting.

"Not good news. He checked for research requests by congressional offices and Natasha Jorgensen's name showed up several times last month. So, Wilson wasn't the only one searching." Spencer's voice sounded somber.

Raymond took another sip of Grand Marnier and felt its golden heat warm his throat. "She could have just ordered the searches for Wilson."

"Maybe. But we'll need to see what's on Jorgensen's computer. That will tell us what she really knows."

"Agreed. By the way, my guy accessed earlier phone records for Gary Levitz and there were lots of calls to Jorgensen. Several of them after Fillmore had his first conversation with Levitz. That's a big loose end, and you know how I feel about loose ends. Another good reason to check her computer."

"Damn," Spencer swore, his voice disgusted.

"Let's see what we find. Then you can check with the committee to see how they want to proceed with Jorgensen. You already know how I feel. Not that I have a vote."

He chuckled softly, the brandy protecting his throat.

Spencer snorted. "You might as well have. I'll get back to you by tomorrow on that."

"Oh, yeah. I assume you want us to resume watching the Malone woman."

"I think we need to, even if they're just casual acquaintances. Maybe they ran into each other by accident on the canal."

"I don't believe in accidents," Raymond sneered. "Unless I cause them."

"Who will you put on Malone? Your main man is on Jorgensen."

"I'll keep an eye on Malone. We already know she's got a pretty regular schedule working for Senator Russell. I'll start tomorrow."

"Field work again?" Spencer said, a slight tease in his voice. "Be careful. And you'd better not use the Maytag uniform again."

Thanks to the brandy's protective layer, Raymond was able to let out a loud laugh.

Wednesday evening

I stepped off the escalator onto the Eastern Market Metro plaza. At twenty minutes past six o'clock, rush hour traffic still clogged the avenues bordering the plaza. Peter had cheerfully excused me from this evening's pre-reception hostess duties so I could meet with Loretta Wade for what I'd phrased as a "research dinner."

Turning my back on the familiar and famous coffee chain at the south end of the plaza, I headed toward the section of Eighth Street where the weekend market always set up. Crossing over Carolina Avenue, I noticed the surrounding cafes were already packed. I hoped Loretta Wade had made a reservation at that restaurant; otherwise, we'd be standing in line at the corner bakery and sharing deli sandwiches on a bench in the plaza.

I'd already explored the other stretch of Eighth Street when Danny and I came to sample some of the cafes across from Barracks Row. A Cuban cafe, a sports bar, and several interesting boutique shops were all mixed together with more cafes along the street. Side streets were filled with lovingly restored townhouses. Gentrification had come and gone. I still remembered when it was called "yuppiefication." The end result was still the same. The turn of the century rowhouses were filled with an ever-changing stream of Washington wannabees. Few, if any, of the original residents remained.

Noise greeted me before I pushed open the door and stepped inside the tavern-style restaurant. All the tables were full in the patio section, and it looked like the inside café was packed. I scanned the crowded scene and noticed an African-American woman waving to me across the patio from a small table beside the screened windows. I wound my way around the tables and chairs, the smell of hops and dark beers tempting me. I spotted a patron's Guinness and my mouth watered.

"Over here, Molly," the woman beckoned me forward.

"Loretta?" I smiled when I reached the table.

She nodded. "Have a seat. I already ordered a beer. I hope you're not a teetotaler, because you won't like this place."

"No worries, there," I said with a laugh as the waiter came up. "A pint of Guinness, please."

"A woman after my own heart." Loretta relaxed back into her chair and observed me.

Her close-cropped haircut sculpted her head perfectly. Not every woman could wear her hair like that and look attractive. On Loretta Wade, it worked. Her high cheekbones and huge dark eyes dominated her striking ebony face.

"You know, you still look like your pictures from years ago, Molly. How'd you escape the toll that time takes?"

Don't be so sure. "Looks are deceiving, Loretta. The wear and tear is on the inside, trust me."

Loretta gave an amused sniff. "Isn't that the truth. None of us escapes unscathed."

Curious that she'd run a search on me, I joked, "Don't tell me Google has file pictures from all those years ago?"

"No, but remember where I work," Loretta said with a smile. "I've got all the *Washington Post* files on digital now. No more of that microfiche nonsense."

The waiter set my Guinness before me with a flourish, complete with a little shamrock design in the foam. *"Sláinte,"* I said, trying to remember the Gaelic pronunciation as I lifted my glass and took a deep drink of the dark brew. *Ahhhhhhh. Mother's milk.* Loretta saluted me with her amber ale.

Licking the foam from my upper lip, I observed Loretta. I could tell from the length of those long legs under the table that she was tall, taller than I was, even. Long-waisted and very slender. One of those women who probably could eat all she wanted and never gain an ounce.

"Okay, which pictures did you pull from the *Post*'s archives? I'm curious. Please say it wasn't those sorrowful ones after Dave's death." I took another drink.

"No, no," Loretta shook her head. "I got some from those early years when your husband was first in Congress. I was studying for my masters in history at George Washington University then. I hadn't met my husband Gabe yet. So I was still single." A smile tweaked her lips. "Lord knows, that feels like a lifetime ago."

"That's because it was," I said with a laugh. "How long have you worked for the Congressional Research Service?"

She took another sip of beer. "Practically my entire Civil Service career. Started as a researcher and moved up. Thank God, because Gabe died ten years ago, so I've been raising my boys on my own since then."

"You've only got one son at home, you said. Are your other two in college?"

"Michael's finishing his senior year at Cornell, and William's serving in the Navy on the *USS Enterprise,* in the Atlantic." She lifted her chin proudly.

"Whoa, you're to be commended, Loretta," I said, lifting my glass in salute. "You've done a fantastic job. William is serving his country, and Michael is at a fine school. Where's your youngest?"

"Brian goes to Gonzaga." She smiled. "I

had all three boys go there."

I gave her another salute. "Fine school, Gonzaga. Great sports teams too." I took another sip. "Raising kids alone is a hard job, I know. After Dave died, I had to raise my two girls on my own in Denver. It was such a different life for them than what I grew up with," I said, unable to keep the slightly wistful tone from my voice. "Thank goodness, my mother and father visited frequently."

"My dad drove a D.C. city bus until the day he died. We lived up on Georgia Avenue, near Walter Reed Hospital. When my sisters and I were growing up, he used to read articles from the *Post* to us every night. He'd go over the names of all the senators and congressmen and what legislation they'd voted on each week. "You know, my dad used to speak highly of your father," she said with an amused smile. "He always singled out the ones who supported civil rights legislation. Your father was one of them. Bless his heart." She wagged her head. "That was a loooong time ago."

"If I'm guessing right, I'd say you and I are about the same age, which means we were still in school then." I snitched a toasted chip from the bowl in the middle of the table. "I was over in Arlington. Where'd you go to school?"

"Archbishop Carroll. We weren't Catholic, but my father insisted my sisters and I go there."

"Sounds like my father. Both he and my mother insisted I attend Mount Saint Mary's. I had to beg them to let me go to Washington-Lee my senior year. Both my cousins, Nan and Deb, went there and it sounded like a lot more fun than the girls' school."

Loretta laughed. "Fun wasn't on our schedules as far as our parents were concerned."

The young waiter appeared by our table. We ordered a cheese and fruit platter. After munching on the ever-present peanuts, we wouldn't need dinner.

"So, tell me, Molly, was there a particular area that your niece Karen was focusing on? That will help me narrow it down. After we talked, I did a quick check to see which subjects Congressman Wilson was researching and made a list." She reached into a purse beside her feet.

"Why, thank you, Loretta," I said, surprised she'd acted so quickly on my request. "That will make it easier."

"Wilson seemed to focus on international monetary policy and banking regulations.

That covers a lot of ground. Do any of those topics match what Karen was researching?"

"As a matter of fact, yes. She left notes on her daytimer. I know that sounds kind of weird. But it looked like she was keeping track of any legislation that involved banking or monetary policy."

"Do you know why?"

"No, not exactly. Just that she was keeping track of it. That's why I was curious about Congressman Wilson's searches. Did any of those topics cover legislation? You know, like legislation being considered by any House subcommittee?"

Loretta frowned at the list. "No, I just did a cursory check on general topics. But I can run a more specific search when I get the chance. See if he was looking at any legislation."

The waiter reappeared then with a bountiful platter of rich and aged cheeses, crackers, and fresh fruit. Loretta and I started sampling the aged cheddar, perfect with the beer. And a rich brie, slightly melted and warm from the oven. Heavenly.

I savored the creamy fattening delicacy, closing my eyes in enjoyment. "Ummmmmmmm, this is so good, it's sinful."

"Don't I know it. But my doctor said to

cut back on those rich cheeses, so smack my hand after two more slices."

"I'll try to remember, but no promises," I said, then took a big sip of Guinness. "Listen, Loretta, I don't want to burden you with extra work. I imagine you've got your hands full supervising staff and keeping track of all those congressional demands."

"You got that right, Molly," she said, handing her glass to the waiter for a refill.

I quickly drained mine and followed suit. At this rate, I'd be drinking tea and nibbling apple slices all day tomorrow so I'd look good in Samantha's lingerie gifts Friday evening.

"Just take a look when you have a chance," I said, slicing a thin wedge of bright orange cheddar. My cholesterol was climbing just looking at it.

"Will do. Any other sub topics?" Loretta bit into a Brie-filled cracker.

"Now that you mention it, see if he did any searches on the Epsilon Group or a European financial minister named Holmberg. Ambassador Holmberg."

Loretta looked at me sharply, clearly forgetting the remaining Brie cracker in her fingertips. "Was Karen researching the Epsilon Group and Ambassador Holmberg?"

I met her gaze and was surprised by the intensity. "Yes. I found references to both of them in her daytimer. Why? Did Congressman Wilson research them too?"

"No. Wilson didn't. But I do know someone else who was researching them." She glanced away, but not before I noticed a tightening of her jaw.

I waited until the waiter placed both our beers in front of us before speaking. My gut had already told me who Loretta was talking about. Celeste Allard. The sweet young staffer from Congressman Jackson's office — Karen's former office — who'd helped search e-mail files for me last spring. That was when I was convinced Jackson's chief of staff, Jed Molinoff, was involved in wrongdoing. Celeste had done many searches for me until her young life ended in a freakish accident on Maryland's Eastern Shore.

"Was that person Celeste Allard?" I asked quietly.

Again, Loretta trained her intense stare on me. "Yes. Did you know Celeste?"

I nodded sadly. "Yes. We met after Karen's death. She called to tell me that Jed Molinoff was acting strangely — searching Karen's desk and removing her computer. Celeste was convinced Molinoff was trying to hide something, and I was too. I'd seen Molinoff in action at a reception, and I didn't trust him." The remembered pain of losing my niece flowed through me again, bringing the remembered anger. "Bastard," I hissed.

"I agree with you. He was a son of a bitch. I heard enough about him from Celeste. I'd met her when she first came to the Hill." Loretta shook her head. "She was so bright and sweet and kindhearted. I made it a point to look out for her. Give her advice. You know, take her under my wing, I guess. And she had to work with those snakes over there in Jackson's office."

I knew immediately to whom Loretta was referring. "Larry Fillmore, right?" I let my opinion fill my voice. "Celeste told me how he was watching her at the office. And again when she went down to Records. He was another bastard."

"Oh, Larry Fillmore is a real piece of work," Loretta sneered. "I used to know his ex-wife, before he drove her out of town."

"I heard about that from a friend who keeps an ear out for Washington gossip. I remember her updating me last spring on Fillmore's tawdry reputation."

Loretta gave another disgusted sniff. "Tawdry is putting it mildly. That man had been transferred from one job on the Hill to another until he landed at Congressman Jackson's office. I cannot believe he's Jackson's chief of staff now."

"Neither can I. Celeste filled me in on his background. She also told me Karen got Jed Molinoff to transfer Fillmore from Jackson's office about a month before her death. Let's just say he didn't get along with the female staffers."

"That doesn't surprise me, given what Celeste said about him. How then did he get back into Congressman Jackson's good graces after being let go?"

"Apparently Jackson never knew about it. Molinoff handled everything. And when Karen died, the first thing he did was bring Fillmore back on board." I frowned into my beer glass. "Celeste was convinced Fillmore was brought back to spy on everyone. And he certainly made her life difficult."

Loretta's expression hardened. "He did, indeed. Listen, Molly, I'll be glad to help you find any information you need for Karen's research. As our own little tribute to two fine young women that left us too soon. Way too soon."

I looked into Loretta Wade's eyes and saw the same light of determination I felt inside. I lifted my glass. "Thank you, Loretta. To

Karen and Celeste."

Loretta lifted her glass. "To the good ones. And to hell with the bastards."

I'd drink to that any day.

FIFTEEN

Friday

I stepped out my front door into the summer morning's embrace, delighted that the humidity wasn't as noticeable as it had been when I was running earlier. I'd left plenty of time for my morning stroll to the Russell mansion, so I could make some personal calls. Once I arrived at my office, e-mails and messages would be nonstop.

Slipping the cell phone from my purse, I continued down the steps to my front walkway. I was about to press Samantha's name on my directory when the phone rang in my hand. *Samantha.* "Hey, you were reading my mind," I answered. "I was about to call you. How're you doing?"

"Surviving," Samantha's drawl flowed as smooth as honey.

"Hang in there, Miss Thing. Where have you and Eleanor been to these last few days? I heard about the D.C. Art League luncheon

237

and the dinner with her book group. Oh, yes, and another fundraiser charity. One of the churches, wasn't it?"

"Yes. That was just the first two days. Since then, Eleanor and I have attended two concerts, one at Kennedy Center and another at Lisner Auditorium. Luncheons for the United Way and Children's Hospital, and another musical interlude at the National Gallery. Oh yes, and a tediously boring reading by some retired diplomat who decided to write his memoirs. I almost fell asleep in that one. I swear, if I'd led as boring a life as he had, I'd never admit it, let alone write about it."

"Culture and charities, how uplifting," I said after I'd stopped laughing. "I'm proud of you, Samantha. I'll bet Eleanor is too."

"I wouldn't say proud. But I can tell I've surprised the hell out of the old dear that I haven't balked at any of her schedules."

I crossed 29th Street, sunlight filtering through the canopy of trees overhead. Morning rush hour traffic stopped at each intersection just long enough for a pedestrian to skip across. Heaven help the slow. Impatient drivers would probably start nudging them along with their front fenders. "Well, I'm proud of you, Samantha. Have you encountered any raised eyebrows?"

She laughed. "Oh, yes, but most of them are smart enough to wait until my back's turned."

"Blow 'em off."

"They don't bother me. I'll walk through snake-filled swamps to make sure my grand-girls aren't subjected to any more vicious gossip. If charity luncheons, symphony receptions, and boring author readings will help, I'll do it. Whatever it takes. By the way, what have you heard from Danny? Or, Double Dangerous, or whatever his nick-name is?"

"Just a text last night saying that he'd pick me up from Russell's house tonight and not to make plans for dinner."

"Oooooo, that sounds like a good start. Listen, sugar, you two have fun, you hear? It's about time you got together. Stop wasting time. Life's too short. I'll talk with you next week."

Samantha clicked off, and I was about to drop the phone back into my purse when I remembered another call. I paused on the brick sidewalk edging 30th Street while I scrolled through my directory. I didn't want to risk tripping over the uneven brick. Pressing Congresswoman Sally Chertoff's office number, I listened to the rings while I meandered slower.

"May I speak with Natasha Jorgensen, please. Molly Malone from Senator Russell's office," I announced when the receptionist answered.

Natasha's voice sounded after a minute. "Hey, Molly, how can I help you?"

"I simply called to see how you're doing, Natasha."

"I'm doing okay. Way too busy, if you know what I mean."

"Oh yeah. Why don't I take you out to lunch next week? You sound like you could use a break from the office. I know I do."

"That's nice, but I usually take lunch at my desk."

"Okay. I'm switching into Mom Mode now. You need a break so you won't burn out. Eating at your desk can be a bad habit. I escape outside every day to Russell's garden for lunch. There're plenty of shady park benches dotted around the Capitol grounds. You can spare a half an hour outside in nature. It'll be good for you, girl."

Natasha laughed softly. "Okay, *Mom.* Why don't we meet Monday around twelve. There are some vendor carts on Pennsylvania Avenue near the National Gallery. We can coordinate by phone. Then we can find a bench."

"Perfect. Monday it is. Oh, by the way, I wanted to start looking at Karen's notes again and try to pick up where she left off. I met the researcher you mentioned from the Congressional Research Service, Loretta Wade, and she's offered to help me. But those categories are pretty broad and there's a ton of information. Do you remember if Congressman Wilson had narrowed his focus at all? I wondered if he left any notes or something."

Natasha paused. "I don't know if he made any notes. If so, he'd have had them in his briefcase. But I do recall I asked him one morning if he was still working on that 'project,' as he called it, and he said he was finishing up."

That caught my attention. "Did he go into any details? The researcher said he was looking at international monetary policy and banking regulations and legislation related to it. Those are pretty broad areas."

"I do recall his mentioning international banking legislation more than once. Several times, in fact. You know, let me look in my desk at home. When I left Wilson's office, I grabbed all my research files that I might need here at Chertoff's office. And I had Wilson's search files on a duplicate storage drive. I'm anal about backing up everything, and I figured he'd want me to. Once I knew I was coming over here, I brought those files with me. Chertoff is on the House Financial Services International Monetary Policy and Trade Subcommittee, so I thought she might be able to use that information. I knew Sylvia Wilson wouldn't need it."

"That was smart thinking on your part, Natasha. I told Sally Chertoff she was lucky to have you."

Natasha laughed again. "Now, you really do sound like my mom. Why don't I make a copy of Wilson's files for you, Molly. I'll bring them to you when we have lunch on Monday, okay? Unless you need them for the weekend. I could send it to Russell's office today."

"No need. I'll get it from you Monday. I've already got plans for the weekend."

"Did your man check her computer yet?" Spencer asked, as he stood beside his office window. The last of morning rush hour traffic still clogged Pennsylvania Avenue below. The U.S. Capitol lay many blocks ahead, the tip of the Pennsylvania Avenue spear.

"He got into her apartment yesterday. Went in while she was at her office," Raymond's scratchy voice came over the phone. "He copied all her e-mails and also copied the storage drives she had in the desk drawer. He's taking a good look and will get back to me later today."

"Will he be able to go over all that by then?"

"Depends on how much there is. But it shouldn't take too long, because he knows how to filter through a lot of the crap and find what we're looking for. By the way, did you hear anything from the others?"

"Nothing definitive about Jorgensen. Some were a little 'reticent,' shall we say, about another termination so close to the last ones." Spencer didn't try to disguise the disdain in his voice.

Raymond snorted. "Sounds like they're getting queasy. I'll call you when I know more."

"I'll be at a dinner for Ryker, so send me a text."

"Will do."

I scanned the tabloid sheet as I stood in the doorway leading outside to the Russell garden. Cicadas buzzed their sultry August drone, the humidity building as the late-morning heat climbed. It would be in the upper nineties again today. Hot and humid. *Dog days of summer at their finest,* I thought as I sipped my coffee and smiled at the *D.C. Dirt's* story.

Newly appointed Congresswoman Sylvia Wilson appeared quite agitated when asked about the photographs taken of her late husband Quentin and his paramour *in flagrante delicto.* Sylvia Wilson hotly denied that she had anything to do with the photographs and professed shock that anyone could think she would threaten her cheating husband with the evidence in a divorce. The *Dirt*'s sources report that police found no blackmail message on Quentin Wilson's computer or in his residence. So who then ordered the surveillance photos? The *D.C. Dirt* is curious, indeed. If anyone knows, the *Dirt* is listening.

The creak of the wrought iron gate that opened into the driveway sounded from the rear of the property. I spotted Albert beckoning the familiar caterer's truck to roll down the driveway. Tonight would be the last of the formal dinners. Next week, only one reception remained before Senator Russell returned to Colorado for the Congressional August recess. Thank goodness, these smaller dinners didn't require my extra hostess assistance like the Senator's large receptions. Danny and I would be entertaining ourselves tonight.

Late Friday afternoon

Raymond set an iced coffee on the glass table beside his patio chair and retrieved the ringing cell phone. Trask's number flashed. No name. "What'd you find?" Raymond asked.

"Nothing in the e-mails. Just office or personal business. But the last storage drive was filled with research files. Monetary policy, international banking regulation, recent financial legislation introduced into committees and subcommittees. Looked exactly like the files we found on Wilson's computer. Jorgensen obviously made copies."

Raymond closed his eyes and rested his head on the cushion behind him. The ice had started to numb his throat. Just a little. Maybe he didn't have to sweat with the hot coffee after all, especially on a summer afternoon. "That's what I was afraid of."

"I figured. Now that we've found the smoking gun, what's next?"

"Well, they know what my recommendation is, but Spencer says some of the others are getting squeamish about a third action."

A deep chuckle came over the phone. "Why am I not surprised?"

"Keep track of her for now. As soon as I hear something, I'll let you know. By the way, will you have time to put up that camera? I wanted to start with the Malone woman tonight."

"I got it mounted this morning. Right across from Malone's house. I was the cable guy. Everyone's used to those trucks. It's all ready to go. I already checked the video feed in your office."

Impressed with Trask's efficiency, Raymond laughed softly. "Good job. I'll head over to the office now and get settled in. Then I can see what Ms. Malone is up to this weekend."

"Prepare to be bored. She's a workaholic. Whenever I checked on her last spring, she'd leave for the office early and not return until later at night most of the times. The rest of the time she'd run out in the neighborhoods. Another time, she drove out to Virginia towards Vienna. Visited friends, it looked like. That's all."

"Good. I like boring. I'll take a book with me," Raymond said with a laugh . . . until his cough started.

Friday evening

I checked my watch as I logged out of my computer: 5:35. Danny should be calling any minute. A buzz from my cell phone showed a text message. Danny, of course.

Almost finished?

I smiled. He was always one step ahead of me. Maybe he really could read my mind. *Scary.* I texted "Ten minutes, max." With luck, it wouldn't be a lie. Now all I had to do was hope that Peter wouldn't waylay me with a question on my way out of the office.

Glancing into the ornate mirror on the wall beside the bookcase, I checked my makeup, grabbed my purse, and locked the office door behind me.

Scanning the hallway, I didn't spy Peter anywhere. So far, so good. The catering staff was making much food-preparation noise — mixers whirring, voices calling over the clatter of metal pans. Entertaining at its height. I'd grown so used to the accompaniment, I thought of it almost as background music.

I walked toward the dining room and spied Aggie and Ryan arranging the table, while Bud the bartender set up the bar at the end of the formal living room. Aggie glanced up, spotted me, and gave a smile.

"Seeing all of you busy worker bees, I

know I can leave with a clear conscience," I teased as Aggie walked my way.

"Would you like me to get you a glass of Sauvignon Blanc before you leave? Bud's got everything set up."

"No thanks, Aggie. I've got a date tonight, and we've got dinner plans. He'll be here any minute."

Aggie's slow smile started. "Well, you have fun, Molly. You definitely deserve to take a break from the Senator's entertaining. All those politicians can be tiresome."

"Isn't that the truth," I said, knowing full well Aggie would be more than interested in tonight's dinner guests. Senator Dunston, chairman of the Senate Banking, Housing, and Urban Affairs Committee, and his wife were Senator Russell's main guests, along with the next two senior members of the committee. Whether Aggie was still playing a spook's role or not, she'd hear a great deal of information over the dinner table tonight.

"I know you'll manage to enjoy yourself, Aggie," I said with a knowing smile.

Just then, I heard Luisa's voice calling my name. I turned and saw Danny standing in the doorway and my pulse did a little skip.

"I think I won't be the only one, Molly," Aggie called after me as I hastened to the door.

I smiled as I walked up to Danny. Luisa had already scurried back to the kitchen, her Cheshire cat smile firmly in place. "Hey, there. How was your trip?"

"Great, if you like being stuck in meetings with a bunch of guys all day," Danny said as he slipped his arm around my waist, guiding me through the doorway.

"Well, at least you weren't dodging bullets or some such," I joked as Danny closed the mansion front door behind us.

I didn't get to say anything else, because Danny pulled me close, his mouth on mine before I could say more. The heat of his kiss took my breath away. *Hungry.* I must have dropped my purse because my arms went around him before I knew it, melding my body to his.

Slowly, Danny raised his mouth from mine and whispered. "We'd better get to the car before we're arrested." Releasing me, he snatched up my purse and hurried me down the front steps.

To hell with dinner. I was ready for dessert. Ravenous, in fact.

Sixteen

Saturday

Traffic noise. A truck rattling down the street. Car horns. Light slowly filtered through my eyelashes. Morning light. *Was it morning?* I wasn't sure. Enclosed in the cocoon of Danny's embrace, I wasn't sure of anything else. Just us. Curved against each other, a perfect fit. Somehow I always knew it would be.

Skin against skin. Warmer than warm. And something else, something I hadn't felt in a long, long time. *Safe.* I didn't recognize it at first. Such a strange feeling. After all this time.

I felt Danny's breathing change, as if he'd sensed my awakening. I moved against him, just enough to get his attention.

"Good morning," his husky voice whispered against the back of my neck.

"Saturday or Sunday? I can't remember." My movements deliberate until I felt the heat of his response.

His hand found my breasts. "Saturday, all day."

I molded myself against him, and his very warm thigh slid between mine. I said nothing more.

Sunday afternoon

Raymond blew out a stream of cigarette smoke as he glanced up from the book in his lap to the video monitor screens on the desk. Nothing moving in front of the Malone house. Not even a pedestrian. Wait . . . a guy walking his dog. Raymond took another drag on his cigarette and returned to the novel. Good thing he'd brought something to read.

His cell phone sounded, and he grabbed it along with a throat lozenge. Recognizing Trask's number, he popped the lozenge into his mouth before answering. "You were right. Good thing I brought two books with me."

Trask laughed. "I told you, she's a workaholic. Nothing exciting."

"Well, she's got something exciting going on this weekend. She showed up here with a guy on Friday night. They started kissing on the front step, then they went inside, and that's the last I've seen of them."

Trask snickered. "Well, well, Ms. Malone's got a boyfriend."

"I'll say. They even had food brought in. A catering truck showed up from some restaurant Friday night, and Malone and her boyfriend haven't come out since." Raymond inhaled deeply, felt the burn.

"Good. Maybe he can keep her occupied and out of our way."

"Let's hope so. What's happening with Jorgensen?"

"The same as last weekend. She's out with friends; they're over here near East Potomac Park, watching some rugby teams."

"No sign of meetings with the Congresswoman or working at the office?"

"No, just normal weekend stuff."

Raymond glanced at the video monitor and straightened. "Well, I'll be damned. They've come up for air. Tee shirts and shorts, looks like they're going for a run . . . yep, there they go down P Street."

"I'll let you know if anything unusual shows up over here. Otherwise, I'll check with you tomorrow. Any word from Spencer yet? I see plenty of opportunities to take care of her. Easy."

"Not yet. You never know with that bunch. They've got a lot of people to answer to. Apparently more have joined on the upper end. No telling what they'll decide."

Trask snorted. "Translation: No guts for a preemptive action. They'll regret it. In that case, there's no need for me to waste any more summer weekends watching Jorgensen. I could be out on the boat."

Raymond chuckled. "Don't go too far."

I looked up at the night sky and spotted the familiar summer constellation — Orion. It was hard to make out the stars with all the city lights around. Back in Colorado, it was far easier to find the perfect spot to stargaze in our mountains, even along the darkened roads at night. Oftentimes, I'd pull my car over to the side of a canyon road, douse the headlights, and stare into the black skies above. We saw the same constellations out West that the Easterners did, but from a slightly different angle. And there was another important difference: in Colorado, the stars appeared larger. Being thousands of feet higher in altitude allowed Coloradans to witness a vast canvas of stars, sparkling in the night skies. Far easier to stargaze there than it was here in the midst of a big city surrounded by streetlights, headlights, and miles of suburban sprawl.

Danny shifted beside me on the chaise lounge, and I nestled closer, my face resting on his bare chest. There in the darkened privacy of my small enclosed backyard, we relaxed in one another's embrace. Our long-overdue weekend of exploring our passions and each other was winding to a blissful close. Tomorrow was Monday and the regular world awaited. But there was still tonight. And tomorrow, and the day after. And next weekend beckoned in the distance.

"What are you thinking about?" he asked.

"How good this feels."

"Ohhhh, yeah." He picked up my hand, kissed it, then placed it on his chest again, covering my hand with his.

"I'm just glad we found each other again. Thanks to the sleaze rag." I laughed softly against his skin.

"I always had a feeling we would."

"Danny, the odds of that happening were impossibly low. With all the millions of people in this area? Crazy."

"I know. But I still had a feeling we were meant to be together." He pressed his lips to my forehead. "Plus, I still remembered that first kiss all those years ago."

I smiled. "So did I."

I felt his soft laughter beneath his skin. "I could tell. And believe me, *that* memory kept me warm through a whole lot of cold nights in God-forsaken hellholes."

I pictured Danny huddled in some jungle, rain pouring down, afraid to close his eyes and give in to sleep. His stories from last May still haunted me. Treacherous jungles and deserts. Killers hiding in both.

"I'm just glad you survived all that, and we found each other again." I slid my hand over his warm flesh. The mosquitoes might be eating us alive, but we were oblivious.

Danny stroked the back of my hand. "I have to admit, I've often wondered what would have happened if we'd gotten together after high school. You know, run away and gotten married."

"You mean, after my father had you arrested? He'd have gone ballistic, trust me. It would not have been a storybook ending."

Danny laughed. "Yeah, you're probably right. But what if we'd met in college? You know . . . after I got back from Nam and you were going to grad school like you said you wanted to do. History, right?"

Brother, this man's memory amazed me. "God, Danny, I can't believe you remember all that."

"I remember everything. Plus, I've got a good imagination." He laughed. "Still, it could have been good. Providing you hadn't met Dave in college, that is."

"Boy, you do have a good imagination.

You forget what it was like when we were that young. We would have fought like cats and dogs. Dave and I did. I'll bet you and your wife did too. Admit it."

"Ohhhhh, yeah."

"You remember what we were like in our twenties and thirties, don't you? Convinced we were right about everything?"

"Don't remind me."

"I mean . . . Dave was mellow, and yet we still fought. You and me? We would have torn each apart."

I felt Danny's laughter ripple beneath my fingers on his chest. "Yeah, you're right," he said after a moment. "But the make-up sex would have been glorious."

We both laughed so hard, the next door neighbor's dog began to bark.

SEVENTEEN

Monday

"Here, Molly, let me empty this pot, so I can start another," Luisa said as she bustled into my office, coffee carafe in hand.

"You're making me an offer I can't refuse, Luisa, especially on a Monday morning," I replied, extending my oversized ceramic mug.

"Peter came in at six thirty this morning, and he and the Senator started working in the library. Casey and Albert just about finished off the pot." She shook the last drop into my mug. "There you go. Now you can return to those spreadsheets while I get back to the kitchen. Caterers are coming at two o'clock."

"Oh, yes, the last summer reception tonight. I'll be ready," I said as she hurried from my office. I suddenly realized I'd forgotten to check Peter's updated list for Senator Russell's schedule. Usually I would check first thing Monday morning when Peter posted it. But considering this past weekend, I figured I was lucky to remember my name.

I clicked back to recent messages this morning and found Peter's list. Tonight would be a reception for various Colorado manufacturers and energy producers. And the last scheduled entertaining before he left for the rest of the August recess. I scanned through tonight's guest list, noticing there were several names I was unfamiliar with. Businessmen and women, entrepreneurs, university researchers. Russell was known to invite a varying guest list to some receptions. Stirring the pot. "Cross-pollinating for ideas," he called it.

Returning to the spreadsheet, I tabbed through the columns and rows, entering the figures on another of Peter's rental properties. It was a newer townhouse in Alexandria, Virginia. The high cost of Metro Washington–area real estate still amazed me. I remembered years ago when that area of Alexandria was first developed.

The familiar strains of "Hotel California" sounded beside my coffee mug. Classic Eagles. Loretta Wade's name flashed on my phone screen.

"Hi, Loretta. What's up?"

"Hey, Molly. I know you're as busy as I am right now, but I wanted to tell you that I had a few minutes before I left Friday night and did another scan. I was curious. This time I looked for who else had requested searches similar to Quentin Wilson's. And I think you'll be interested in the answer."

"Okay, I'll bite. Who?" I took a big drink of coffee while I waited.

"Larry Fillmore."

I gulped down the coffee quickly. Images of Larry Fillmore's smirking face appeared in my mind. "Fillmore, huh? Congressman Jackson is on the House Financial Services Subcommittee on International Monetary Policy and Trade. So maybe he wants them for the congressman. Strange that Fillmore would do the search himself. I've heard he's really full of himself now that he's Jackson's chief of staff. Usually he'd use one of his —"

"Research grunts," Loretta finished for me, her voice sarcastic. "Yeah, I wondered why he was doing it himself. So I did another scan, which I can do because I know the system, and I found Fillmore had first looked at research requests and who made them. In effect, he was searching the searchers. That's how he found out what files they were looking for."

I pondered that for a few seconds, my brain cells slowly coming back online from a weekend of blissful sexual indulgence, thanks to strong coffee and even stronger memories of that bastard Larry Fillmore. I still held him responsible for driving Celeste Allard out of her D.C. apartment, forcing her to escape to a house on the Eastern Shore — only to die in a freakish accident.

"You know . . . anytime I see Larry Fillmore interested in something, it gets my attention. I can't help it. It's a knee jerk response."

"I figured. That's why I wanted to point it out. And you mentioned your niece Karen was researching the same topics. I wondered if maybe Jackson had assigned Karen a special project or something. Maybe Fillmore is following up on it for the congressman."

Everything Loretta said made sense. Logical. Yet, it didn't resonate. "Funny, Karen never said Jackson asked her to research anything special, and she would have mentioned it. I recall her saying she was following her instincts and her late father's personal notes. Her father, Eric Grayson, took over my husband's seat in the House after his death in 1983, remember? Eric moved

Karen and his wife, Cheryl, to Washington that same year." Remnants of old memories crept to the edges of my mind, waiting to escape. I shifted the subject, and they slunk back to the bushes. "You may remember Eric Grayson."

"Yes, I do. He was a fine legislator and extremely thorough. I know because I remember him coming to the Library of Congress. I was researching there, and I remember seeing him sitting at the tables later at night, reading and making notes. Very studious."

That caught my attention. "Now you've made me curious. Karen said her dad's notebooks had entries that indicated he was interested in that organization, the Epsilon Group. She checked into them and found they're a think tank of sorts and seem to specialize in international financial policy and banking issues. That's why I asked Celeste to check into them after Karen's death."

"Yes, that's exactly what I learned about them."

"Is there any way you could find out what other topics Eric Grayson was researching? I know it was years ago, and your records may have been purged of anything like research requests."

"True, but there may still be a way. Thank you, Molly. You've given me a puzzle to solve, and I dearly love puzzles," Loretta said, amusement in her voice.

"Happy to oblige. And thanks in advance. You may not find anything. I'm simply following my instincts like Karen was."

"That's good enough for me. Our instincts always know something we don't." She paused. "Speaking of instincts, you remember hearing about that staffer who was found dead in Texas? The one who was providing those damn drugs to Congressman Wilson."

"I sure do. The news said he worked for the Congressional Research Service. Did you know him?"

"Ohhhh, yeah. Gary Levitz was his name. I was his supervisor, and my instincts told me he was involved in something on the side. Had to be. His car was way too expensive for a staffer's salary. Plus, I'd see him outside talking on his cell phone several times a day." She gave a disgusted sniff. "I took Gary aside a few months ago and told him he'd better think twice about whatever he was doing in his spare time because it was affecting his job here. He didn't pay attention, unfortunately."

I debated exactly what to say. "That was

good of you to try and help him, Loretta. But it sounds like that guy was on his own path, and it led only one way — down."

"That's the truth. I even saw him talking to Larry Fillmore last week. I was crossing the street and saw them outside the building. That's when I knew Gary was headed for a bad end. Anyone who gets close to that cretin Fillmore regrets it. And sure enough, Gary went missing a few days later."

That got my attention, and my instincts gave a little buzz. "I wonder if Gary was supplying Fillmore with drugs."

"No, I don't think so. Fillmore may be a manipulative bastard, but he's not stupid. He'd never jeopardize his chief staffer position by getting involved in something like that."

"You're right. Listen, my other phone is ringing. Call me if you find anything interesting."

"Don't worry, I will. Talk to you later."

Her phone clicked off as I clicked on my office line. Samantha's name and number were flashing. "I figured you'd be calling me this morning," I said as I grabbed my coffee and leaned back in the desk chair.

"Of course, sugar. I tried your personal line, but it was busy, so I thought I'd leave a message. Now that I've entered Mother

Superior's order, I'll have to live vicariously through the sexual adventures of others." Samantha's drawl infused her words with a wickedly suggestive tone.

I snickered. "Well, I won't give you a detailed rundown."

"Sugar, I would never be so rude as to ask. Just tell me if it lived up to your expectations?"

I laughed out loud, then took a sip of coffee before answering. "You mean was it good? As in scream-out-loud, best-sex-I've-ever-had good? *Ohhhhh, yeah.*"

"Thank *gawd!*" she exhaled. "I didn't think your Double D, Danny Dangerous, would disappoint. Tell me, where did you two go for dinner? You said he had plans."

"That, he did. A catering truck arrived at the same time we got to my house from Senator Russell's. They brought all sorts of delicious food in covered pans and set up everything before they departed. Danny and I never left the house all weekend. Except late Sunday afternoon, when we went out for a run." I sipped my coffee and listened to Samantha laugh.

"Mercy, I'm all aglow just hearing about it," she said in an outrageous Southern Belle voice. "I simply love it. Shacked up all weekend. You're a woman after my own heart, Molly. Fine food, fine wines, and fine loving. Oh, you did have wine, didn't you? I hope Danny relaxed the 'no wine' rule for this weekend."

"Yes, he did. We had an unbelievable reserve Cabernet. I don't want to know what it cost."

"Stop being an accountant. It's about time you were properly taken care of, sugar. Your dear Dave and that politico Frank just weren't up to the task."

I snickered. "You make me sound like an urban renewal project."

"You're a project, all right. And you're definitely difficult. Few men would even bid on it."

This time, I nearly choked on my coffee.

"It's the truth, sugar. I was about to give up on you until Danny showed up. You two have a connection so strong it gives off sparks. I can feel it. Clearly, you two are destined to be together."

"You're such a romantic. You know I don't believe in destiny. Danny and I were just lucky to find each other after all these years. I suppose I have the *D.C. Dirt* to thank for that. Maybe I'll buy a subscription and stop mooching Casey's."

"Make fun all you want, Molly. But you know I'm right. I know you, girl. There's a romantic inside you, and you're just afraid to let it out. Now you can. Don't argue with me."

"What? *Me,* argue with the all-wise, omniscient Miss Thing? *Never!*"

"I certainly hope Danny plans to stay in town for a while. Now that he's got added incentive to do so."

"I think so, but I never really asked. It must have slipped my mind. Funny how sex clouds the brain."

"Amen to that. Well, I think I've had as much vicarious stimulation as I can handle right now, given that I need to meet Eleanor and her friends for another charity luncheon. This time in that patio off the Smithsonian's Sculpture Garden."

I checked my watch. After eleven already. "Thanks, I needed the reminder. I'm meeting Natasha Jorgensen for lunch near the Capitol. We're having burgers or hot dogs from a truck. The girl is a workaholic, but I convinced her she needed to take a break."

"That's like the pot calling the kettle black. Say hi to Natasha for me, please. I've got to go put on the habit before I leave."

"Give Mother Superior my best," I said with a smile as I clicked off the phone, closed out of the spreadsheet, and reached for my purse.

■ ■ ■ ■

It was well past noon and the August sun was beating down, relentless, reflecting off the asphalt of Pennsylvania Avenue as Natasha and I walked away from the food vendor cart. Dog Days of August. The sun glare was so intense, even my sunglasses couldn't filter it all. My clothes were drenched already. No wonder my dry cleaning bills were so high.

"There're some benches over there under the trees," Natasha said, pointing across the street.

I took a bite of my New York–style hot dog with all the trimmings as I walked. Couldn't resist. "Yummmmm," I said, savoring. "I forgot how good these are."

"Yeah, it's delicious, but I'll probably regret it by late afternoon," Natasha joked, licking mustard off the edge of the long bun.

The traffic light changed just as we approached, so we scurried across the intersection as the mechanical birdy chirped its warning to the vision-impaired. Trees and shade beckoned ahead. Natasha and I fairly raced down the sidewalk and escaped into the welcoming shade.

"Just in time. My scalp was getting sunburned," I said as we walked toward an unoccupied bench. Two women had just vacated it.

Others had sought the shade, too, sitting on benches reading, eating lunch, talking on cell phones. Several yards away I spotted a group of elementary-age children sprawled on the grass as two women passed out soda cans. It was too early for most schools to be in session, so I figured it was a church- or civic association-sponsored tour. The kids had the telltale uniform-color tourist bandanas.

Tourists were everywhere. Piling off tour buses parked along Pennsylvania Avenue and adjoining streets, walking behind tour guides who managed to cross streets backwards while giving verbal instructions to their groups at the same time — in English and in multiple foreign languages. Tourists rolled by on large-wheeled touring vehicles, paraded in quiet disciplined lines and in unruly noisy bunches. Climbing the Capitol steps, posing for pictures around the fountains, traipsing along the avenues, and perched on the stone borders edging the National Gallery licking ice cream cones and popsicles.

Two men passed us, both carrying what looked like iced coffees. "Whose idea was it to have lunch outside today?" I joked.

Natasha swallowed her last bite of hot dog then grinned at me. "That's okay. Even though the heat's brutal, it still feels good to get away from the office and into fresh air. Even with the humidity."

I polished off the last of my hot dog as we claimed the bench. Opening the cap of my icy diet cola, I gulped down the cold liquid. Cold had never felt so good. "Ahhh, now I feel better."

Natasha followed suit, upending her lemon-lime drink, then exhaled a long sigh. "Boy, I needed that."

"Have you heard any more about your friend Gary?"

"Yeah, his mother sent me a card thanking me for the flowers I sent to their home in Minneapolis. He had a lot of family there, so I'm glad his parents weren't alone. They're still broken up about Gary dying from a drug overdose." She exhaled a long sigh.

"I can't imagine how hard that is for them," I commiserated. "How about you, Natasha? How's it going at Chertoff's office? Are you feeling more settled in?"

"Oh yeah. They treat me like I've always been with them. It's been an easy adjustment. Of course, I have to study up on

Congresswoman Chertoff's committee and subcommittee work. But the August recess gives me time to catch up. The congresswoman is back in Iowa. So I have the time. Good thing, because I have a lot of late-night reading every night. That reminds me." She reached into her purse and withdrew a small key-ring-sized computer storage drive and held it out. "I copied those files for you. I may be studying some of them myself, since Chertoff's subcommittee deals with International Monetary Policy."

I took the little green storage drive and dropped it in my purse. "Thanks, Natasha. I appreciate your help. I'll take a look in a few days." No way was I going to research dry financial legislation while Danny was in town. We had plans every evening this week. Data searches could wait until Danny was off consulting . . . or whatever he did while away. Remembering my earlier conversation with Loretta Wade, I said, "Congressman Jackson is on the same subcommittee as Chertoff. In fact, last spring Sally mentioned that she and Jackson were working on something together. Were they drafting a bill?"

"Well, they were, but it looks like it's stalled now. So, I'm not sure where it's going. Seems support has waned, if you know what I mean." She eyed me before draining her lemon lime.

"I have a good idea. Someone with more seniority has shifted his support. But with both Chertoff and Jackson behind the bill, you might see some movement. I've heard Jackson is a rising star."

Natasha smiled slyly. "Apparently. He's a good guy. And a damn good congressman."

A woman walked past us, talking loudly on her cell phone. An older man squatted on the grass and threw breadcrumbs to the pigeons. Within a minute, he had an eager, cooing audience.

Flying rodents, my father used to call them. He hated the pigeons and insisted that one of them would wait for him to walk from the Capitol every evening, then swoop down and deposit something on his expensive felt fedora. In an era when every gentleman wore a hat outside, this was a grievous annoyance. I always made sure I didn't smile while I pictured my dignified U.S. Senator father shaking his fist at the feathered miscreant as it flew away.

Curious, I asked, "Have you ever worked with Larry Fillmore? Since he's Jackson's chief of staff now, I figured both your offices might have collaborated."

This time, Natasha's smile turned contemptuous. "That slime? I met with him earlier this spring when Wilson and the Ohio delegation were going to Omaha for meetings. What a jerk! And for the record, there's *no* collaboration with Larry. It's his way or nothing." Natasha glanced at her watch. "Darn it. It's over a half hour already. I'd better get back."

"Me too," I said, as we both rose from the bench.

"Thanks for thinking of me, Molly. I appreciate it," Natasha said with a big smile. "You've been involved in this hothouse a lot longer than I have, and I forget how easy it is to burrow into work at the office and not come out until dark. It felt really good to be outside, even with the heat."

"We'll do it again in the fall. Until then, we can always meet up while we're running by the Canal. It's a lot nicer in the mornings."

"Great idea." She gave me a smiling wave as she walked away.

"Take care," I called as I started in the opposite direction. Tossing my empty soda can into a nearby metallic trash bin, I headed toward Pennsylvania Avenue to catch a taxi. I needed a cab to return to Russell's office. Too bad Georgetown wasn't on the metro line. Years ago, Georgetown's longtime residents, dubbed the cave dwellers, gave a thumbs-down on metro stations in their neighborhoods. Foggy Bottom was the closest, and it was several blocks from the Russell mansion. A nice walk most times of year, but not in the Dog Days of August.

Trask leaned back in a metal chair beneath the café table's blue-and-white-striped umbrella and sipped his beer. Tucked away in a rear patio, Pennsylvania Avenue traffic noise was muffled and barely reached the sheltered bistro. Most of the D.C. lunchtime crowd had returned to their offices by now, and not many tourists ever discovered the small cafe. That was another reason Trask liked it. He flipped open his cell phone and pressed a familiar number.

"We didn't have to wait for long," he said when Raymond's scratchy voice answered.

"Tell me."

"Jorgensen met with Malone for lunch today near the Rayburn Building."

"You gotta be kidding. The two of them *together*?" Raymond chortled. "*Christ!* Talk about dumb luck."

"It wasn't luck," Trask corrected. "I figured Spencer was going to cancel Jorgensen's surveillance because nothing showed up. But I still had a feeling about her, so I watched where she parked this morning while she went running. Then I got into her car and bugged her cell phone. That's how I learned she was meeting Malone. Jorgensen called her and said she'd be late for lunch."

"Were you able to get there in time?"

"Yeah, with the cycle. They grabbed hot dogs off a cart on Penn then found a shady bench near the Rayburn Building. So I started feeding pigeons on the grass nearby."

"Were you able to overhear anything?"

"Nah. Too much traffic noise. But I did see Jorgensen hand Malone a storage drive, a green one, exactly like the one I found on Jorgensen's desk with Wilson's files."

"No shit? *Damn.*"

"Yep. That's what I say. Now that ought to be enough for even those weak sisters on Spencer's committee."

"Don't bet on it. Spencer said the new members nearly peed their pants when they heard about the second termination. Too close to the first one."

"But Jorgensen knows everything Wilson did. She can cause trouble."

"Not quite everything. She wasn't in that library room like Wilson was, eavesdropping on Ryker and Holmberg. Spencer is betting Wilson didn't share that part with his staffer."

Trask made a disgusted noise then took a deep drink of beer. Even out of the sun, no one could escape the heat. "You know, it sounds like old man Ryker is slipping. Starting to make mistakes. What in hell was he doing, talking about that stuff in a public place?"

"I hear you. Spencer said he damn near choked when Ryker told him about it. Ryker was just lucky he was still in the hallway when Wilson slipped out of the room, otherwise he'd never have known Wilson was eavesdropping."

"And he's lucky they have us to clean up their messes." He looked up at the young waitress and smiled. "I'll take the quesadillas."

Raymond chuckled. "By the way, that was great work, Trask. I'm gonna put you in for a medal."

"Screw the medal. They can add it to my fee. I've got my eye on a bigger boat. Maybe I'll check it out this weekend. If they're not gonna worry about the Jorgensen chick, then I sure as hell won't."

"Let's wait and see what Spencer says. The fact that Ms. Malone may have a copy of Wilson's files won't set well. Last spring she was using the Allard girl to check some of the same information Wilson found out.

But Malone stopped snooping after Molinoff took that dive off his balcony. Everything was all tied up, nice and neat. And now this. *Crap!* I'll call Spencer now. He's not going to be happy Malone is involved again."

"What is it with this Malone woman? I understand about her niece last spring. That one needed to be messy, and Malone found her. But you once said that Malone has a past history with Spencer's group. I know Eric Grayson was her brother-in-law and all that, but she wasn't even here in Washington when I did that job. So, what's the rest of it?"

"It's . . . complicated."

Trask recognized Raymond's tone when he was deliberately hedging. He snickered. "Okay. Let me know what Spencer says."

"At minimum, I think he'll want us to find out what's on those files Jorgensen gave Malone. So you'll probably be checking her computer tomorrow."

"Roger that." Trask clicked off his phone, just as a platter of quesadillas was set before him.

EIGHTEEN

Tuesday morning

"Did you make it to that meeting on time?" I asked as I grabbed a small yogurt from the fridge. "You had to leave so early, I was barely awake when you kissed me goodbye."

Danny's voice came through the phone. "By the skin of my teeth. There was an accident on Wisconsin Avenue that slowed me down. Whoever scheduled a meeting at six thirty in the morning deserves to be shot."

I hurriedly set my half-filled coffee cup in the kitchen sink. I was running late because of an early morning call from my daughter informing me of her promotion at a Denver law firm. "Where are we going for dinner tonight?"

"I haven't decided yet. Probably somewhere close so I can get you back fast and take your clothes off."

I laughed as I dropped the yogurt into my purse and headed out the back door. "I like the way your mind works. Hey, I'll talk to you later. Gotta run to the office now."

"Call me later."

I clicked off my phone as I slammed the back door and gave it the usual final pull to lock it. Old wood was swelling with the humidity. I'd have to give Peter my "To Do" list for fall maintenance. Hurrying around the side yard, I skipped down the steps to the sidewalk as Bruce meowed his lazy "goodbye."

Peter leaned inside my office doorway. "Hey, Molly, I'm going to need you to print off some files for me. I'm still knee deep in studying financial legislation that's coming up in the Senate Subcommittee on Security and International Trade and Finance next month. Unfortunately, I'm running behind schedule."

"Sure," I said as I rose to follow him down the hallway. "Are you and the senator still leaving for Colorado this afternoon?"

"We've moved it up to late morning," he said, rounding the corner into his library office. "That's why I'm hurrying now. This recess came at just the right time, believe me. The senator and I are buried. We'll be studying the whole time we're there."

"You're the second staffer who's told me

that this week," I joked. "Natasha Jorgensen is buried in trying to catch up on some of that same legislation for Sally Chertoff's House Subcommittee on International Monetary Policy and Trade."

"I feel her pain. Chertoff told me she and Randall Jackson were working on a bill involving regulation. She didn't go into detail." He picked up a pile of papers from his inbox with one hand and started sorting through more papers spread out on the desk. "Where is that flash drive? Ah, there it is." He snatched it up and handed it to me. "Please print out the files on international financial and development institutions, okay?"

"Sure thing." I was about to head back to my office when an idea slid forward from the back of my mind. "You know, Karen was researching subjects similar to that before she died. And I have some files on a flash drive at home. If you'd like I could copy them for you. So you'll have them while you're burrowed in for the recess."

Peter looked up quickly. "Hey, I'd love to see anything Karen was researching. She was the best." He checked his watch. "But you'll have to hurry up. We've gotta leave for the airport in forty-five minutes. Luisa and Albert are out on errands, so Casey is driving us. Can you get back by then?"

"No problem." I gave a dismissive wave. "Let me start these files printing while I run back home. See you in a few minutes." I hurried from the library, telling myself that research was research, right?

"Listen, Nan, I'll have to call you back," I said into my cell phone as I ran up the steps to my front door. "I'm back at my house now. I have to get something for Peter then race back to the office before he leaves for the airport." Digging my keys from my purse with my free hand, I shooed Bruce out of my way as he came racing toward me.

"Okay, call me later. Bye, bye. Shoo, Bruce, I don't have time to pet you," I said, clicking off my phone as I slid my key into the front door.

Bruce meowed loudly in feline frustration as I pushed open the door and hurried inside the house. Dumping my purse on the foyer table, I hastened over to the small desk in the corner of the living room. Spying the green storage flash drive Natasha had given me yesterday, I snatched it up when I noticed something. A hum. A computer hum.

My desktop computer was on. That

couldn't be. I always turned it off after using it; I didn't want to risk forgetting the old desktop and leave it running. I usually used my laptop and only used the desktop for personal files, family files, and such.

I stared at the darkened monitor screen and saw the telltale green light blink. It was on. I reached for the mouse and moved it on the mouse pad. The screen brightened immediately, revealing the "My Documents" file.

My pulse skipped a beat. I never left my files open when I shut down. The old system was on its last legs, so I didn't want to risk a hard close. I stood up from the desk, and that's when I noticed the bottom desk drawer was halfway open. Something else I wouldn't do. I always closed drawers so they were neatly flush. An anal accountant trait, no doubt, but one I always performed.

And I always pushed the desk chair back into place. Now the chair was sitting a foot from the desk. I wouldn't leave it sitting out like that.

My pulse sped up.

I pulled open the lower drawer and this time my breath caught. Instead of being filed neatly with her other papers, Karen's old daytimer was placed on top of the files in the drawer. I picked it up and saw the three blue flash drives that Celeste Allard had given me last spring — before she died in the gas explosion. They were in the bottom of the drawer where I'd left them.

My heart started pounding. Was I imagining things? Had I simply forgotten to shut down my computer? Left the chair sitting a foot from the desk? Forgotten to close the desk drawer?

Maybe you could have accidentally left the computer on and forgotten the chair — but you haven't opened that lower desk drawer with Karen's things in over a month.

My heart sank to my stomach. I frantically looked over my shoulder, halfway expecting to see an intruder standing behind me. Panicked suddenly, I ran for the front door, snatched my purse, and raced outside into the front yard. I stood beside the terraced gardens, my heart beating so fast I could barely breathe.

What do I do now? Call the police? What do I tell them? That I found my computer on and the drawer open? They'd think I was crazy. Was *I crazy? Was I simply imagining things?*

I tried to slow my breathing and order my thoughts. I needed to get back to Peter. But I couldn't just ignore what I'd seen. *Had* I seen anything?

No, you didn't, my practical side spoke up,

sounding remarkably like Sober-and-Righteous. *You're simply acting like a little kid, scared of the dark. What's the matter with you? Running out of your house like that. You're a grown woman, not a child. You're imagining things that aren't there.*

The Hell she is! shouted Crazy Ass.

Just then, Bruce's insistent meow broke into my tangled thoughts. The big tabby stood at the edge of the yard meowing loudly. It was a strange meow, strident and hoarse. I'd never heard him make that sound before.

"Stop it, Bruce, not now," I said, trying to dismiss him so I could think straight.

Instead of being silenced, however, Bruce meowed even louder, pacing back and forth. Annoyed at myself for acting like a scared child and aggravated at Bruce, I walked around the side of the house as Bruce raced ahead into the backyard.

"All right, all right, I'm coming. But you'd better not show me some bird you just killed."

Bruce ran straight to the back door. He meowed once, then sat down and stared at me.

"Is that what all that noise was about?" I asked him as I approached. "You want me to go inside and open a can of tuna? Good

Lord, Bruce. You are more than spoiled. I never should have started feeding —"

I broke off admonishing Bruce as I reached for the door handle with my keys. I stopped and stared. The door wasn't completely closed. Not the way I had closed it this morning, giving it an extra yank to hear it click. Of that, I was absolutely sure. No doubt in my mind.

TOLD YOU! Crazy Ass screamed. *Now, do something!*

I did. I ran back to the front yard as fast as I could, frantically digging my cell phone from my purse. I forced myself to calm down as I flipped open the phone and pressed Danny's number.

"Hey, there," his warm voice sounded.

I took a deep breath. "Danny . . . could you come over to my house? Right now, I mean?"

"Molly, what's the matter? Where are you?"

"I'm at my house . . . I came back a few minutes ago to get something for Peter . . . and . . . and I think someone came in while I was gone. The back door wasn't closed properly like I always do. I yank it until it's shut and . . . and it was open. And my computer was on and —"

"I'll be right over. Where are you now,

284

Molly? Are you inside the house?"

"No, no, I'm outside in the yard. I panicked . . . and I ran outside."

"Good. Stay there. I'm coming over now. Have you called the police?"

"No . . . not yet."

"Okay, I'm on Connecticut Avenue right now. I'll cut across and be there in a few minutes. And Molly, don't go inside. Promise me."

"I promise." But my slowly relaxing gut started to twist again.

As soon as Danny clicked off, I found Peter's number and took a deep breath. His brisk voice came on the line. "Hey, Molly, I hope you're around the corner because Casey just pulled up front."

"Peter, go ahead to the airport. I'll e-mail those files to you. I came home, and I think someone got into the house while I was gone this morning."

"Holy crap! Are you sure?"

"Yeah. Whoever it was messed around in my desk, and the back door was partially open. I always yank it shut when I leave in the morning."

"Damn, Molly. Have you called police?"

"Not yet. I called Danny and he's coming over. I'm thinking maybe I scared whoever it was when I came back this morning. I must have surprised him . . . or her. I didn't see anything missing in the living room. But I haven't checked anywhere else."

"Listen, I'll tell Casey. He'll probably want to come over when he returns from the airport. I'm so sorry, Molly. Will you be okay?"

"Yeah, Danny is spending the night with me. No way would I stay here alone after this." I surprised myself with my blatant honesty.

Peter chuckled. "Well, that's the best news I've heard all day. Keep me posted. I want to know what's happening. You want me to tell the senator?"

"No, don't. I don't want him to worry. Maybe later."

"Okay. Talk to you later. I hear Casey beeping outside."

"Fly safe, Peter." I clicked off the phone just as I spotted Danny's car turning into my narrow driveway.

Danny was out of the car the moment it rolled to a stop. "You stay out here, Molly," he said, taking me by the arm. "I'm going to have a look around. Then you can show me what you found, okay?"

"Do . . . do you think he's still there?" That thought froze my insides.

"I don't think so. Sounds like your sudden arrival surprised him and he ran off. I just want to make sure." He leaned down and kissed my forehead. "Don't worry. I'll take care of it."

Danny started toward the front door, and I followed after him despite his admonition to stay put. All sorts of scary images danced before my eyes now. Scruffy criminals, burglars climbing out of windows, running out my front door.

"What do I do if he runs out the door? Scream? Call the cops?"

Danny glanced back at me. I didn't even try to hide how spooked I was. "Come on," he said, beckoning. "Stay behind me."

I obeyed without a word, one of the few times ever.

Danny stepped into the foyer as I followed after. He reached inside his jacket and withdrew a large pistol. Any calming thought that might have hovered on the edge of my mind fled the scene at the sight of the pistol. If Danny brought a gun, it really was something to worry about. I swallowed down whatever scary thought kept popping into my head as we walked throughout the entire downstairs level and then the upstairs. Danny opened closets, pushed back clothes, peered behind furniture, checked windows, looked under the beds. I stood silently watching.

We walked down the stairs and into the foyer once more. "There's nobody here, Molly," Danny said as he holstered the gun. "Like I said, whoever it was took off the moment he saw you return. Now, why don't you show me exactly what you found."

"Okay . . . I came home and walked straight to the desk," I said, retracing my path. "I picked up the flash drive I was looking for and was about to leave when I noticed a humming noise, like my computer was running. But I always shut it down whenever I use it, which isn't often. So I moved the mouse to shut it off, and I saw this."

I demonstrated and watched the screen brighten with the "My Documents" file staring back. I watched Danny's expression change, ever so slightly as he stared at my computer.

"I would never leave any files open. I'm kind of anal that way. Just like I wouldn't leave the chair sitting a foot away from the desk or the drawer half open." I pointed to the lower desk drawer. "That got my attention right away, and when I looked in the drawer, I found Karen's daytimer pulled out from the other stuff and sitting on top." I pointed below.

"Can I see it?" he pointed toward the day-timer.

"Sure. It's just regular office stuff," I said, handing him the black spiral-bound book. "Notes about meetings and appointments."

Danny paged through the daytimer, scanning the pages. "Looks like most office day-timers."

"Yeah, I know. But that's the drawer with Karen's things, and I haven't opened it for over a month, I'm positive. So, when I saw that, well . . . I panicked and ran outside."

"And called me. Good instincts," Danny gave me a little smile as he handed me the daytimer.

"Actually I didn't call right away," I confessed. "I wasn't sure if I was imagining things or not, then Bruce started meowing and —"

Danny did a double take. "The *cat*?"

"It's hard to explain. Come outside and I'll show you." I beckoned as I hastened out the front door. Danny followed, with a puzzled expression. "I know this sounds strange, but Bruce started making a racket like he was trying to get my attention, then he ran into the backyard." I hurried across the small front lawn and around the corner toward the backyard, Danny right behind me.

As if on cue, Bruce himself suddenly ran out of the bushes and accompanied us to the back door. Not a meow to be heard.

"Anyway, he ran up to the door, then sat down. I figured he wanted me to go inside and give him a can of tuna. But when I reached to unlock the door, I saw it like this. Partially open." I pointed at the telltale gap between the door and the frame. "I leave through here almost every morning, and I always give the door an extra yank to make sure it clicks closed. The wood is swollen."

Danny's slight smile disappeared, and his eyes narrowed as he stared at the door.

"That's when I knew it wasn't my imagination. The only way that door would be open was if someone was in the house and came out this way. Someone in a hurry, who wouldn't stop to check the door."

Danny nodded slowly, still looking at the door. Then he glanced at the brick walls above. "You're right. Someone was in your house this morning."

"That's when I called you."

Danny looked at me. "You did exactly right. Now I'm going to make sure this doesn't happen again." He gave me a quick kiss then pulled out his cell phone. "You need a high-level security system, and I know exactly who can install it." He glanced down at Bruce, who was sitting a few feet away, observing us. Inscrutable kitty expression intact. "Good job, Bruce. You got yourself a watch cat, Molly. He deserves a can of tuna," Danny said, then pressed a number on his phone.

"Wait . . . I should check with Peter first before you call someone."

"I'm paying for it," Danny gave me a smile. "I'll make sure they send Peter a bill with a discount."

"I don't know . . ."

"Don't even try to argue with me, Molly. I don't want you in this house until it's secured. The intruder clearly knew your routine. Otherwise he wouldn't have tried a daylight morning break-in. Yeah, this is Daniel DiMateo. Put me through to Bennett, please."

I watched Danny talk into the phone and pace the lawn at the same time. I heard all sorts of terms I'd never heard before and guessed they were discussing equipment. But I wasn't really paying attention. All I could think about was Danny's comment: "The intruder clearly knew your routine."

That cold feeling in the pit of my stomach returned. *Who would be watching me?*

NINETEEN

Later Tuesday morning

Raymond looked up from the laptop screen and reached for his ringing cell phone. "That's faster than usual, Trask. What'd you find?"

"Not as much as I wanted. Malone broke pattern and showed up at her house out of nowhere. Suddenly I heard her voice outside, talking on her phone. I barely made it out the back door in time."

"Shit!" Raymond slammed the laptop closed.

"First time that's ever happened. At least I copied the flash drive. And, I put a bug in her living room wall, near her computer. I figured you guys might be interested."

"You figured right. *Damn.*" Raymond lit another cigarette. Half of another was already burning in the ashtray. "Where are you now?"

"I'm in traffic, couple of blocks from your

office. I want to see what's happening at her house. I had to move the van because they're remodeling two houses across the street. Trucks everywhere. But I'm guessing she figured out someone broke in, because I just heard her talking to some guy a few minutes ago. She told him she found her computer on. I couldn't make out anything after that because of traffic noise."

Raymond pushed back his desk chair. "Lemme go take a look," he said heading toward an adjacent room. Electronic equipment filled the shelves that lined two walls of the windowless inner office. Raymond went to the desk with the video monitors.

"She's with a guy, all right. Looks like the same one who was over there last weekend. They're standing in the front yard."

"No wonder I'm not picking up any conversation. What're they doing out there?"

"Just talking. Wait a minute . . . a car's pulling into the driveway. No, a Suburban. Black Suburban. Who the hell is this?" He reached over and manipulated a control on the board. Leaning over, he peered at the screen. "Can't read that logo. Boyfriend is walking over . . . uh, oh. Hurry up, Trask. You need to see this."

"I'm a block away."

Early Tuesday afternoon

I leaned on the living room doorjamb, watching Danny and the security specialists maneuver about my home. I sipped some of the fresh coffee I'd just made. My single contribution to the proceedings taking place. Another man sat at my ancient desktop computer, examining files, financial accounts, even the family photos. I might not know much about security systems, but even I could tell the system they were installing was way above average. I'd seen a neighbor's being installed in Colorado years ago, and it only took the man about an hour to set it up.

My office cell phone rang inside my purse and I grabbed it. Casey's name flashed. I retreated outside to the back patio to answer.

"Hey, Molly, Peter told me what happened. I'm on my way to your house now, as soon as I can get out of this traffic and across the bridge."

"No need to hurry. Danny's here with some guys he's hired to install a security system, even as we speak."

"Wow, that was fast. I'd like to see the security system. Have you called the police yet?"

I paused. "No, I haven't. I . . . I didn't

want to come across as some panicked female who was imagining things. All I found was my computer on, a drawer halfway open, and the chair pushed back. And, the back door partially open. Now, I know those things are suspicious because I know my routine. But the cops would think I was a nut. So . . . I'm not calling it in."

"Okay. I see your point."

"And nothing is missing. I think I scared the guy away when I came home unexpectedly. So, I was lucky, I guess."

Funny. I didn't feel lucky.

"Even so. I feel better you're getting a security system installed. That's a pricey neighborhood, so thieves regularly check it out to see which houses are vulnerable. Now yours won't be. I'll see you in a few minutes."

Danny stepped out onto the patio as I clicked the phone off. "Casey will be here in a few minutes. He'd like to see the system."

"Good. I want to make sure he's in the loop."

"How's it going in there?"

"They're almost finished. Bennett found something you need to see. First, do you know who rented this townhouse before you? Or was it privately owned?"

"I don't know. But I could find out easily. Why?"

Danny beckoned me inside. "Come on in. But, don't say anything."

"What?"

Danny silently led me into the kitchen then down the hall and into the living room where Bennett and his team, as Danny referred to them, had gathered. One man still sat at my computer. Another man held what looked like a metal box.

Bennett held out his palm as I approached. I stared at the small object in his hand. I glanced at Danny with a puzzled expression. He pointed to the object, then pointed to the wall directly above my computer. Then the man sitting at my computer held up a piece of paper with the words "Listening device."

I stared at the words on the paper, and felt the cold claim my insides again. All those scary images that had danced through my head earlier returned. A strained whisper escaped. I couldn't help it. "Oh, my God . . ."

Bennett quickly turned to the man beside him and dropped the object into a metal box. The man snapped the box shut.

"Now, it's clean," Bennett pronounced. "Signal's gone dead."

"Now we can talk," Danny added.

Still stunned that someone had been eavesdropping on me, I could barely think, let alone talk. "My God, was that thing here when I moved in four months ago?"

"It looks like a newer model, plus there was no dust or dirt accumulation," Bennett answered. "So we're thinking it was put there fairly recently. But we can't be sure. It may have been placed last year when someone else lived here."

I glanced at Danny. "That has to be it. There's no reason anyone would be listening to my conversations. I'm not a politician. I just work for one." I shook my head, trying to remember all the times I had friends in or . . . or Danny. *Oh, my God! Danny . . . last weekend.*

I glanced at Danny, and he must have read my mind because he started to smile. "I hope they enjoyed themselves."

I closed my eyes. "Oh, my God . . ."

"What's important, Ms. Malone, is no one will be listening to you now. And no one will enter your house unless you allow them. We've secured both front and back doors, all the windows, and the basement area. In fact, we've sealed off the basement since you told us you never use it. And the door locks have been replaced with our special digital entry system. We've also installed our control system in the hallway. I'll explain the emergency call function."

"They even repaired that back door," Danny said with a grin.

"What happens if one of my relatives or a friend drops by when I'm not here and they look in the windows? Does that set off an alarm or something?"

"I'll show you. Plus, we've installed video cameras around the outside of the house, so our technicians will already be alerted if someone starts snooping around your house. Friend or foe."

I was more than impressed. "Wow, you guys certainly are thorough."

Bennett actually smiled; first time I'd seen a trace of one. "Our job is to keep you safe, so you feel safe, Ms. Malone. Feel safe and be safe. Now, let me show you what we've done. Let's start at the front then we'll work our way throughout the house."

Bennett walked toward the front door, and I followed dutifully after him, flanked by Danny. *Feel safe and be safe.* Good words. Now if I could only believe them.

"They've killed it," Trask said, tossing the earpiece onto the desk. "Who the hell is Prestige Systems, anyway?"

Raymond scanned through a list on his computer screen. "Gotta be privately paid consultants. Their website only has an e-mail address and a phone number for messages. My bet is the boyfriend knows them. Or maybe one of the senator's staff. Who does the senator's security?"

"Probably the same agency that staffs all their events. Preferred Professionals. They supply all the servers and wait staff. But I learned they have a security company as well. The caterers are separate. Not connected."

"Preferred Professionals . . ." Raymond leaned back in the chair and took a drink of hot coffee. "Rumor has it that years ago half their serving staff were CIA spooks."

"Still are, from what I've heard." Trask drummed his fingers on the desk. "Maybe Prestige Systems is their company."

Raymond shook his head. "My gut says no. Something tells me these guys are private and they specialize. But check on Preferred Professionals again, okay? See what you can find out about their security business. I'm betting they mostly provide security for events and personal protection like Russell's."

"Okay," Trask said distractedly, staring at the monitor screen again. "Look . . . they're showing Malone the video system. *Damn!* They've locked that place down tight."

"Yeah, they have," Raymond said, observing Trask's annoyance. He couldn't resist adding to it. "You're not getting in there again."

Trask didn't respond, but his answer was written on his face. Extreme aggravation. Trask wasn't used to being thwarted.

"I know you're pissed, but it was bound to happen sometime, Trask. You've been doing these jobs for years. Random roll of the dice. You know, statistics." Raymond grinned, just because it would annoy Trask even more.

Trask just shot him a look.

"Anyway, it sounds like you got what we needed. You copied the file. I'll take a look and share it with Spencer. And that stuff in the desk drawer didn't sound important. What was it again? Flash drives from the Allard girl?"

"Yeah, and they looked like the same ones I'd taken from her apartment and that house on the Eastern Shore. But I wanted to take a closer look at the Grayson girl's daytimer. She had notes written all over the thing. Lots of initials. I'd only started going through it when Malone came home."

Raymond took a deep drink of his hot cof-

300

fee, thinking. "That doesn't sound like much. Notes on a daytimer, that's all. Office stuff, most likely. I'll tell Spencer, but I think he'll agree."

"So, what do you think they'll do next?"

Raymond took a long drag on his cigarette, felt that burn, then blew out a slow smoke stream. "Oh, I know what they'll do. Once they hear about Malone discovering the break-in and her new security system, they'll shut down all direct surveillance. Reduce the risk. We'll check occasionally, just to keep an eye on her. But they won't authorize any actions. You can bet on that."

Trask smirked. "I figured as much. They're making a mistake though. If she starts snooping around again, no telling what she'll find."

"Well, right now, Malone hasn't found out anything really. Just general information. More research on international monetary issues. Big yawn. Nothing important. Nothing that ties Ryker to anything specific. Not like Wilson did. Wilson overheard Ryker mention one of the banks involved in the transfers. Then Holmberg asked about the specific bill going through committee. The Jorgensen girl doesn't know any of that, either."

"How can you be sure?" Trask looked

dubious.

"Because she would have been spilling her guts to someone in Chertoff's office by now. Ryker's made a lot of enemies over the years. There are plenty who'd love to have the ammunition to take him down." He flicked the ash off his cigarette.

"He'd better be more careful then. More slipups and he'll hand them all they need. Better keep his mouth shut."

Raymond snorted. "He's a politician. He's incapable of that." Trask stared at the monitor again. "Listen, why don't you just stay loose for a couple of days until we hear from Spencer on what the group decides. Then, you can take off for a week on your boat. Maybe more. Who knows?"

"Yeah, sounds good," Trask said absently, staring at the screen.

Curious at Trask's concentration, Raymond said, "You've been doing stakeouts too long, Trask. Stop staring at that screen and get out of here."

"You're right. It's just . . ."

"Just what?"

"I don't know . . . something about Malone's boyfriend. Something about him looks familiar. I haven't had a good look at him. He's usually got his back to the camera or his head turned away."

"How many years were you in the Marines, Trask?"

"Five. Why?"

"And how many years were you a mercenary?"

"Twelve. What are you getting at?"

"And you've been working with me for seven years. You've met thousands by now, Trask. Just like I have. Same story. After awhile, we think we recognize everybody. They all start reminding us of someone. Usually someone we've killed."

Trask returned his attention to the screen. "Or wanted to."

"Yeah, that too. Now get out of here and start planning where you're gonna sail."

Trask finally smiled. "Roger that."

TWENTY

Later Tuesday afternoon

Danny slipped his arm around my waist as we watched the Prestige Systems team back their black Suburban out of my driveway. "Feel better?"

I did, actually. It was hard not to, after seeing the complex system Bennett's team had installed. "Yeah, I do. Thank God." I turned to Danny. "And thank *you.* I wouldn't have known where to find a company like that. And Peter surely wouldn't."

"You would have probably asked Casey, and he would have put you in touch with someone," Danny said as we walked toward the front door where Casey was standing, staring up at the video cameras Bennett's team had installed. "But they wouldn't have been as good as these guys. And that's what I wanted for you." He kissed my temple. "I want to keep you safe, Molly."

Even that small touch of his warm mouth

stirred me. Now that fear had finally slunk back into the bushes, I was finally able to feel other sensations. Desire, for one. Pressed close to Danny, desire rose quickly. Only the presence of Casey kept me from suggesting Danny and I go inside.

"I'm impressed," Casey said as he walked toward us. "That is one helluva system they've installed for you. What'd you say their name was again?"

"Prestige Systems," Danny answered. "I can give you their number. You need a recommendation."

Casey grinned, "I'm not surprised. Well, done, Double D. I have a feeling Peter Brewster is lucking out and doesn't even know it." His smile evaporated quickly. "I'm just glad you won't be vulnerable anymore, Molly. These neighborhoods are way too tempting for thieves."

"I'll say." Danny nodded in agreement. "You were lucky you came home when you did and scared the son of a bitch away. And you were sharp enough to notice someone had been inside. Other people might not have picked up on those signs."

"Yeah, I guess. It's just . . ."

"Just what?" Danny prodded.

"I still don't understand why a thief who's taken the time to watch my schedule so he could break in would spend time looking at my computer files or poking around in the desk drawers."

"Maybe he was looking for money?" Casey suggested.

"Yeah, maybe," I agreed. "It's just . . ."

Danny studied me. "I can tell something else is bothering you, Molly. What is it?"

"The bottom drawer had Karen's office daytimer pulled out from the files. Celeste Allard said Molinoff was angry when he couldn't find it in the office. Also in that drawer are the flash drives where Celeste put all of the stuff she was researching for me. They're on three flash drives."

Both Danny and Casey stared at me. "I thought Celeste was simply doing e-mail searches for you," Danny said.

"That's right, but she also researched that organization I told you about, the Epsilon Group. You remember when we went to see that speaker?"

Danny nodded. "Yeah. And I remember how boring he was. Don't tell me you have his speeches on those flash drives?"

That made me laugh. "To tell the truth, I only skimmed through them earlier this summer. It's mostly research notes on economic issues. Stuff like that."

"I think it's more likely the thief opened

that drawer looking for your financial information," Casey said. "Probably hoping to find credit card statements or bank statements with your account numbers."

That resonated. Nothing like money to get someone's attention. "Good Lord, you're right." I shook my head. "Of course, that's what he was looking for. I don't know what I was thinking."

"I think you're still spooked by what happened today," Danny added. "And, be honest. It's only been a little over four months since Karen's murder. A lot of bad memories."

Casey grimaced. "I'll say. Another reason to be glad you've got this new system. This is a dangerous city." He glanced at his watch and started walking away. "I'd better get back to the house. See what else Peter wanted done today."

Danny and I followed him toward the sidewalk. "Do me a favor and shut down my computer system, please," I remembered to ask. "I'll be in tomorrow."

"Who did the system for the Russell house, do you know?" Danny asked him. "Or did you handle it?"

Casey opened his car door. "Matter of fact, I didn't. The system was already in place. I checked it out and everything was working perfectly. I thought we had top of the line, until I saw this." He glanced back at the house. "I'm going to suggest to Peter that he take a look at this one. After what happened here, I'll bet Russell will want an upgrade."

"I'll bet you're right," Danny agreed.

Casey started his car. "Why don't you two go out for a late lunch or early dinner. You deserve it," he suggested with a smile, then pulled out onto P Street.

"I was about to suggest that very thing," Danny said, as we watched Casey drive down the street.

The mid-afternoon summer sun filtered through thick maple trees bordering the sidewalk. Cicadas droned overhead, high pitched, in the heat. Maybe a shady patio not too far away, with an icy pitcher of sangria and lunch leftovers. Gourmet fare. Then a fast pace back to Fortress Malone.

I slid both arms around Danny. Public display of affection, be damned. "If I'm not mistaken, you made a delightfully lewd suggestion earlier this morning before the criminal interruption."

Danny smiled that slow smile that always set my pulse racing. "You're reading my mind."

"Turnabout is fair play," I said as I lifted my mouth to his.

Tuesday evening

Raymond sipped the aged scotch as he watched Pennsylvania Avenue traffic far below. Headlights flashed on, taillights bright in the early evening. "Have you heard from Ryker yet?" he asked the man standing beside him at the large window.

"Oh, yes," Spencer replied. The large diamond in his ornate gold ring caught the overhead light as he lifted his glass to his lips. "He was not happy Malone discovered the entry this morning and the bug. I reminded him that none of the actions would have been necessary if he hadn't gotten careless a month ago. If he hadn't shot off his mouth where Wilson could overhear, we wouldn't have had to clean up after him."

Raymond chuckled. "I bet that shut him up."

"Yeah, it did. For the time being. He's getting full of himself now that the bill passed his committee." Spencer drained his glass, moving away from the wide window as he walked across his spacious corner office to the beige leather chairs clustered about a coffee table.

Raymond followed after him. "I'm not surprised. Ryker delivered his committee. Now, Dunston has to deliver the Senate committee." He sank into buttery soft beige leather and leaned back into the chair. "Do you foresee any problems? Dunston seems to have burrowed into the chairmanship."

Spencer picked up the cut glass decanter on the table and poured more amber liquid into Raymond's glass. "Not really. Dunston's made sure the bill is treated as bookkeeping issues mostly. International money transfers. Common daily occurrences. Nothing interesting."

Raymond admired the liquid gold in his glass. Light sparkling off that outshone the flash of Spencer's enormous diamond to his way of thinking. "Except in those cases, the transfers would be done by your banks." He smiled at his old comrade, then took a drink of nectar and felt the gold coat his throat.

"Amen," Spencer grinned and lifted his glass. "He who holds the money, makes the money."

Raymond stared toward the window, lights from the Washington Mall and monuments shone in the distance. Early evening twilight. "We were lucky today. With Trask, I mean."

"Ohhhh, yes." Spencer settled into the chair across from Raymond. "I promised

Montclair there'd be no contact with Malone. You're going to keep an eye on her. Just occasionally. That's enough. Nothing obvious. As we said before, she doesn't know anything. Not really. Those Wilson files are simply reports of monetary policy. I assured Montclair she knew nothing."

"Let's hope it stays that way. I told Trask he could take some time off. Go sail his boat, take a break."

"Tell him he can start his break in Europe." Spencer reached inside his jacket and withdrew a silver storage drive and placed it on the coffee table. "We need Trask to deliver this to our man in Stuttgart. We want a personal delivery on this matter. You can tell Trask we'll book him through London first, then Paris. I don't imagine he'll mind an extended stay in Europe. The tourists will be leaving for home soon. Leaving Europe to the Europeans once again." He grinned.

"I think he'll enjoy it. The sailboat can wait a few weeks. He wants to buy a bigger boat anyway. So he might as well go shopping along the south of France." Raymond laughed until his cough started. But the glorious molten gold soothed the annoying tickle away.

"Vive la France," Spencer agreed, lifting his glass.

ABOUT THE AUTHOR

Bestselling mystery author **Maggie Sefton** was born and raised in Virginia. She grew up in Arlington, a stone's throw across the Potomac River from Washington, D.C. Maggie's hometown has always had a special hold on her, which she blames on her lifelong fascination with Washington politics. Maggie swears she's been watching politicians since she's been old enough to read the *Washington Post*. Author of the bestselling Colorado-based Kelly Flynn mysteries (Penguin), her books have spent several weeks on the *New York Times* bestseller list and the Barnes and Noble bestseller list.